HIND POCKET BOOKS

THE MAHARAJA'S MAN

Other titles in this series

- Maharaja
- Maharani

THE MAHARAJA'S MAN

RAKESH BHAN DASS

assisted by
ANKUR DHIR

HIND POCKET BOOKS
An Imprint of Penguin Random House

HIND POCKET BOOKS

USA | Canada | UK | Ireland | Australia
New Zealand | India | South Africa | China | Singapore

Ebury Press is part of the Penguin Random House group of companies
whose addresses can be found at global.penguinrandomhouse.com

Published by Penguin Random House India Pvt. Ltd
4th Floor, Capital Tower 1, MG Road,
Gurugram 122 002, Haryana, India

Penguin Random House India

First published in Hind Pocket Books by Penguin Random House India 2019

10 9 8 7 6 5 4 3 2

The views and opinions expressed in this book are the author's own and the facts are as reported by him which have been verified to the extent possible, and the publishers are not in any way liable for the same.

ISBN 9789353491055

Printed at Repro India Limited

www.penguin.co.in

FSC www.fsc.org MIX Paper from responsible sources FSC® C047271

This is a legitimate digitally printed version of the book and therefore might not have certain extra finishing on the cover.

Contents

What He Believed in:

Myself to me my Kingdom is
Such perfect joy therein I find.
No, worldly ware my mind can toss,
To me no gain, to me no loss
I fear no foe, I scorn no friend
I dread no death
I fear no end

Family History

The author of the best selling book *Maharaja,* Jarmani Dass was born on October 4, 1895 at Sultanpur Lodhi, Kapurthala, Punjab. His father Diwan Daulat Ram was the Private Secretary to Maharaja Jagjit Singh. At the age of 33, he fell a victim to court intrigues and died as a result of a poison administered to him by jealous colleagues. He died at Mussorie.

He was survived by his wife, four sons and a daughter. The eldest son Diwan Sureshwer Dass became the Chief Justice and later on the Home Minister of the State. For his justice and philanthropy he came to be known as "Motianwale Sarkar".

The next in line was Diwan Wilayati Ram who rose to be the Superintending Engineer at in the then PEPSU. Then there was Diwan Mankeshar Dass who joined the Baroda State as Superintendent of Police. His sister was married to Gurdas Mal who belonged to a very noble aristocrat Bedi family of Dera-babanank. The youngest was Jarmani Dass.

The eldest brother Diwan Sureshwer Dass showered his love and affection on Jarmani Dass. The young Jarmani was brilliant at studies and played tennis very well as well as chess and badminton.

The entire family's hopes were on him. The absence of the head of the family strengthened the bonds of love which lasted for all times to come. Much later, when Jarmani Dass gave up his job in Kapurthala, his brother Diwan Wilayati Ram suffered a heart attack on hearing this news. He rushed to his brother along with a cardiologist ignoring all consequences. The bonds of love between the brothers were very strong and they never snapped.

Jarmani Dass was a brilliant student and passed his Matriculation examination with distinction from the local school. He passed his Intermediate examination from Randhir College, Kapurthala where he studied French and acquired proficiency in speaking French.

Maharaja Jagjit Singh of Kapurthala was a Francophile and he appreciated it when anyone spoke in French.

Maharaja Jagjit Singh enrolled a number of young men belonging to the aristocratic families for duties as Musahibs. A Musahib's job was to present himself daily at the corridor of the Palace at 7 a.m. These young men were selected on the basis of their merit and personality including lineage, phy sique, intelligence, sportsmanship and genius. The young sters were supposed to report for duty in their spotter dresses and were to be spick and span. The Maharaja planned his days of week for palace, early morning pursuits such as one morning was reserved for cycling, the other for riding and yet another for jogging, long walking. On each morning, the Musahibs present at the corridor had to salute the Maharaja and accompany him back to the palace and then disperse for their respective schools. They were paid rupees fifty each per month as honorarium for this service. Reading, swimming were imposed by Jarmani Dass.

In those days the Maharajas used to send their children for higher education to the well-known universities of England and France. In England, Col. Perrot had been appointed to look after the royal children. Jarmani Dass was also sent to Oxford for higher studies. Col. Perrot, whose house was opposite to his college, took extraordinary care of the young Jarmani. Years later whenever Jarmani Dass visited England, he did not miss to pay his respects to the ailing colonel and his wife. After completing his education at Oxford, he went to Sorbonne University, France, for higher studies in Political Science and French language. His class-fellows were the children of the leading royal families and aristocrats of Europe.

Here he stayed with a French family in which communication was possible only through French. It was a result of staying with such families that he could speak French accurately and fluently. During his first visit to Paris he stayed as a paying guest with Madame Dujob. Her daughter Lilly and son Pierre, were of the same age group of

Jarmani. They did not know a word of English so French was the only language for communication. As a result Jarmani's knowledge of French language became more polished and precise.

He returned to India in 1917 and was appointed Private Secretary to Maharaja Jagjit Singh. Thereafter, Maharaja appointed him Deputy Director of Education and Sports. He held this post for *2* years. Then he rose to the position of the Military Secretary at the age of *27* and afterwards he was appointed Minister for Household Affairs. He held this post till May 8, 1933.

The Khatris of Punjab have reasons to be proud of their inheritance. All the Ten Gurus were Khatris. They occupied high administrative positions during the Mughal and Pathan rule. Akbar the Great, had nine Ratnas (Courtiers) among whom was Raja Todar Mal, a Punjabi Khatri, who is remembered till this day for introducing the land revenue system. Maharaja Ranjit Singh was ably served by eminent administrators and Generals like Diwan Mool Raj and Diwan Mohkam Chand.

In those turbulent days after the death of Maharaja Ranjit Singh when treachery came to be considered a virtue, the Diwans remained loyal to the last. In the long past, out of this main stock emerged a sub-caste called Dhirs which came to settle at Sultanpur Lodhi, near Kapurthala. The word Dhir means courage in Sanskrit. In the hoary past the ancestors of Dhirs must have shown lot of courage so that they began to be called Dhirs. Whatever be their history, the Dhirs of Sultanpur Lodhi lived in the full glare of this newly acquired label.

Jarmani Dass's father, grandfather, great-grandfather and even earlier ancestors were Ministers and Diwans of Kapurthala State. His great-grandfather Diwan Ramjas had been an historical figure. He led the state forces of Kapurthala against the Afghans during the Anglo-Afghan war with such an efficiency and valour that the army chronicles of those days sing paeans of praise for him. He was also a great social reformer of his age. He worked hard to break the narrow caste system prevailing at that time and also made reforms in the marriage and dowry systems. He actively worked to break the caste system among the Hindus and promoted inter-caste marriages. He believed that charity should begin at home. He and his cousins married their daughters in Bedi family of Gurdaspur. It was because of him that Maharaja Jagjit Singh sat on the throne of Kapurthala. The real father of Maharaja Jagjit Singh was a Chopra. Jarmani Dass's great-grandfather Diwan Ramjas signed a contract with this Chopra and transplanted his new born son in the royal family. If he had not made these efforts the throne would have passed on to another branch of the collateral i.e. Maharaja Jagjit Singh the nephew of Maharaja Khark Singh, who had embraced Christianity and renounced the religion, culture and heritage of their forefathers.

How he achieved this goal is lucidly and vividly described in detail in Jarmani Dass's celebrated work *"Maharaja"*. He ruled Kapurthala State for 13 years as a regent because Jagjit Singh was only five years when Maharaja Kharak Singh died. His grandfather Diwan Mathura Dass was sent to London to plead with the Secretary of the State on behalf of Maharaja Jagjit Singh. He did this job successfully and on his return, the Maharaja gave him hundred of acres of land at Sultanpur Lodhi, Kapurthala and its neighbouring villages.

Like Diwan Ramjas, Diwan Mathura Dass was also full of "Indianess". He took with him to London, Gangajali (Holy water of the river Ganges) and his own cook who prepared "shudh" (pure) food for him. His father Diwan Daulat Ram was a Private Secretary of Maharaja Jagjit Singh of Kapurthala. He, being a favourite of the Maharaja, accompanied him to Europe whenever Maharaja went on foreign jaunts. While in Germany, Diwan Daulat Ram received a cable that he was blessed with a son at Sultanpur Lodhi. He, therefore, named his son "Jarmani Dass". He carried the singular distinction of being the only man with this name in India. His wise counsel was very much appreciated by the Maharaja and the common man looked upon him as his true friend. An English gentleman, Mr. Samuel Warring representing a firm Waring and Gillow of London failed to strike a bargain with the Maharaja for the supply of furniture, because of Diwan Daulat Ram's opposition to it. Mr. Warring wrote the following uncomplimentary lines about the Diwan:

"Amongst the persons holding office at the Courts of Indian Princes, the Ministers entrusted with the financial affairs of the Princes were probably the most influential.

Diwan Daulat Ram had known how to be indispensable to the Maharaja."

"As a young man Daulat Ram had studied for a few years in England and passed the Bar-at-Law Examination with distinctions. In addition to this, he acquired all the good qualities of the West. In European company he behaved like a English gentleman, which made a particularly great impression on the Maharaja, with whom he in consequence stood in very high favour."

According to another incident, when plague struck Kapurthala in 1926 Diwan Daulat Ram went from door to door distributing medicines and organised other relief works. Although he was attached with the Maharaja, yet his mind was with the common man. Because of their distinguished services the photos of ancestry of Diwan Ramjas was displayed at Kapurthala Palace which now houses the prestigious Sainik School.

His elder brother Diwan Sureshwer Dass became the Home Minister of Kapurthala. Later he became the Chief Justice of Kapurthala State and came to be called 'Motianwale Sarkar' because of his philanthropic attitude. Like his ancestors he too was proud to be an Indian. His nationalism found flamboyant expression in his book *Glories and Sorrows of India* published in London in 1906. It was banned by the British Government which felt that the book glorified India's past and highlighted its plight under their rule and thus encouraged nationalist activities in India. It undoubtedly made Indians proud of their heritage. The British suspected him for having links with the revolutionaries like Bhagat Singh, Hardial, etc. connected with Lord Harding Bomb case. The suspicion was well founded because he did support the underground revolutionaries, such as Lala Hardial, Devta Swarup Bhai Parmanand and Sher-e-Punjab Lala Lajpat Rai.

His father had died at the age of 33 due to poisoning. His mother Bhagwanti Devi was a very saintly and God-fearing lady who brought up her children on the same pattern. It was her love and care which helped all the four brothers and their sister to grow up into noble personages. They inherited a spirituality that stood by throughout their lives. The widow mother, toured many religious temples. There is a record with the Punjabi Dharamshala at Gaya, Bihar of her visit in 1915. She travelled often to Haridwar, Rishikesh, and Varanasi. She, though, an illiterate house-wife succeeded admirably in managing 1600 acres of agricultural lands at Sultanpur Lodhi. The Maharaja too, took keen interest in bringing up the children.

Diwan Jarmani Dass was a Sanatanist Hindu of Catholic views. He had reverence for all religions, their holy books such as Ramayana, Mahabharat, Quran, Bible, Guru Granth Sahib etc. and the holy places of all religions. He went around the world many times, meeting eminent personalities and visiting places of historical, cultural and architectural value. In spite of his busy schedule whenever he went he paid a visit to holy places, such as churches, cathedrals, temples, mosques, gurudwaras and stupas in the East and the West. He took a special trip to Jerusalem to visit the historical places connected with the birth and crucifixion of Lord Jesus Christ. He went to Morocco, Egypt and other Muslim countries to see the famous mosques such as Sultan Hasan Mosque (Cairo), Al Azhar Mosque (Cairo), Qayrawan (Tunisia), Masjid-i-Juma and Masjid-i-Shah (Isfahan), Iskale Jami (Urkunder, Turkey), Umayyad Mosque (Damascus), Golden Mosque (Baghdad), and Badshahi Mosque (Lahore) etc. and to meet the saintly persons. He visited the historical churches in Munich, London, Paris and other places all over the world and also saw the holy cathedrals and churches at Louvres in France, connected with the Holy name of St. Bernadotte of miraculous powers. He was received twice by His Holiness the Pope and the Vatican who conferred upon him the Grand Cross. He visited Angkor Wat and Angkorthem, the biggest Hindu temples in the far east, situated in Cambodia. He also took a special trip to see the ruins of Baalbek about 30 miles northwest of Damascus where the devotees of the medieval times used to worship the Sun, the Moon, the Stars and the Storms, or other elements of nature.

From the numerous historical places he visited, he collected many objects of arts and paintings of religious interests. He had a Mala (Black Tasbi) from which one could see Mecca and Madina. Black Tasbi is still with the author. With such paintings and art objects he used to enthral his friends and visitors to his house. Besides this he had brought a couple of unique paintings of dancing girls, painted table-clothes, etc. and a Chhankhana – a musical instrument

– producing lyrical sound from Bali Island. He studied the Bible, Quran, Guru Granth Sahib and other religious books – Vedas and Purans, Gita, Mahabharata and other philosophical and classical literature of ancient India. From his trips and visits to these holy places and after the study of the holy books of most of the religions of the world, he formed his own opinion on Dharma. "Gather ye the wisdom of East & West", was his motto. So he believed in taking the best from every religion and giving practical shape to it in every day life. His anti-retinue of servants always consisted of Hindus, Muslims, Christians and Sardars. His favourite was the whole-time Barber Rehme Khan who used to recite the Kalmas (couplets) in the morning while giving him the body massage with scented coconut oil. He left India in 1947. This he thought was the best way to attain eternal peace and happiness. He has himself recorded his childhood experiences."

His mother along with the baby Jarmani Dass visited the shrine of Baba Balak Nath in Kangra valley, now in Himachal Pradesh. There she offered the infant clad in saffron robe and langoti (loin-cloth) with big beads Rudraksha around his neck, a begging bowl in hand and a sash around the waist. After blessing, the infant was given back to the mother Bhagwanti who in return offered five figure amount to the holy Shrine. The priest advised the mother to be always gentle with the baby. Later, on many occasions, the boy wore the saffron robes. Its significance dawned on him. Because of these offerings, visits and saffron robes, something was engraved on his mind which made him a God-fearing man who felt his first duty lay in the service of his fellow men. He never wavered in this conviction throughout his life. Many occasions came in his life when he had to choose between his self-interest and the national interest. He always chose the latter.

All these varied experiences – spiritual and divine – etched a new profile of Jarmani Dass exuding a cosmopolitan outlook who thought in the typical and traditional Indian psyche of saints and sages, savants and seers that this whole world is my country, entire mankind is my family and to do good is my religion. The ensuing couplet by Sheikh Saa'di the Persian poet was the guiding light and motivating force in the life and living of Jarmani Dass.

Minister in Kapurthala, 1919-1933

Take care of the poor and the needy
And remember that the ruler owes his Crown
To the people and the people are the roots
And the Ruler is the tree
And the Tree depends on the roots.
Do not offend the people's feelings
If you do, you uproot yourself.

Sheikh Saa'di, (Persian Poet)

The State of Kapurthala had an area of 630 square miles in Punjab and another 700 square miles in Oudh (U.P.) Its population according to 1901 census, was 3,14,351 and revenue Rs. 13 lakhs. It was an Ahluwalia Sikh State. By the time Diwan Jarmani Dass became a Minister, the population and the revenue must have increased considerably. However, the importance of the State in British eyes lay in its strategic location. Like all other erstwhile States, the British found in

Phulkian State such as Patiala, Nabha, Faridkot, Kapurthala and Maler Kotla a strong bastion of imperialism. At the outbreak of First World War, Maharaja Jagjit Singh placed the revenue of his State at the disposal of the British. At that time it was considered to be fairly a rich State in Punjab. Kapurthala, being the capital of the State, was a mini-Paris with well-manicured gardens and civic plans. The official and non-official buildings had excellent architectural value.

The Kapurthala Ruling dynasty was founded by Jass Singh Ahluwalia and the Ahluwalia Misal. He was a great warrior and contemporary of Nadir Shah Abdali. The State came under the protection of the British in 1809. During the Anglo-Sikh War, the State sided with the British against their compatriots. The then ruler of the State, Nihal Singh, was suitably rewarded and given the title of Raja by the British for rendering valuable service to them against the Lahore Durbar. Another opportunity came the way of the State during 1857 when its Maharaja gave full support to the British during India's first war of independence erroneously called the Mutiny. As a result of the services to the British at this critical juncture, the confiscated States of Bundi and Bithuli in Oudh were given in to the Maharaja of Kapurthala as a gift. During World War I & II, the State was in the forefront in laying all the resources at the disposal of the British masters.

Maharaja Jagjit Singh was the most famous of all Maharajas of North India. His rule covered a span of seven decades. He was a Francophile and a great traveller. In both his pursuits he was ably assisted by Jarmani Dass who was like one of Nav Ratnas in the Durbar of Akbar the Great of Mughal Empue (Emperor). The trails blazed by him were picked up by his fellow princes. Jarmani Dass always accompanied him on those foreign tours. Often the Maharaja was confronted with serious problems, which were solved by him. In Press Conferences in Europe and America, Jarmani Dass answered the questions very ably. He lent sophistication to the Maharaja's tours and travels and put Kapurthala firmly on the map of the world. This small State came to be known all over the world because of the untiring efforts of these two persons. Jarmani Dass always accompanied His Highness Maharaja Jagjit Singh to meet the great personalities like Colossuses Mussolini, Haille Selassie, Churchill, Hirohito, Clemenceau, Hoover, etc.

An Indispensable Asset

Maharaja Jagjit Singh had an insatiable wanderlust. He was given due respect wherever he went. Whenever a political question was asked he used to say "Please talk to my Minister". The Minister-in-Waiting was always referred to in the Press as the Sardar and it was none else than Sardar Jarmani Dass. Due to his bristling brilliance and charming personality he used to be the most popular person in the country visited by the Maharaja and him. He always gave a befitting reply couched in diplomatic overtones. The friendships he developed with V.I.P's became everlasting. Long after his visits, he would receive letters, Christmas and

New Year greeting cards from the dignitaries of the world. He used to visit educational institutions, art galleries, places of cultural interest, factories, farms and historical sites, etc. He made an in depth study of all such places and prepared exhaustive notes. However, Maharaja's interest was different. In 1929, Maharaja Jagjit Singh and party visited Honolulu when he was completing his two-year trip round the world. He expressed a desire to see the Waikkiki Beach and see the Hawaiian Hula dance and the dancing girls. After this visit he had to go to Japan where he had an appointment with Emperor Hirohito. On this occasion he was accompanied by Sardar Mohabbat Rai the other courtier of Kapurthala. The Maharaja tasted the local delicacies and enjoyed the local dances. Jarmani Dass gave the local leaders a picture of the progress his country was making. The "Honolulu Star Bulletin" of October 25, 1929 gave a vivid description of this visit. He, therefore, proved a valuable asset to the Maharaja in his foreign jaunts.

Student at Sorbonne, Cambridge

Jarmani Dass was brought up in a very liberal atmosphere. He had his early education at Randhir College, Kapurthala and higher education at Cambridge. Then he joined Sorbonne University of France. He had lived in democratic England and revolutionary France. Back home when he saw the lewd and luscious lives of Maharajas he felt repulsed. Circumstances forced him to remain in their service but he never liked their ways of life. Almost all the Princes were fanatics. Maharaja Jagjit Singh of Kapurthala used to spend nine months abroad in a year, where he spent millions on fun and frolic with total unconcern for the public back in his State. When he returned home he always brought a fresh wife or a mistress whose physical attributes and feminine charm he used to know beforehand. Next year the old wife used to be discarded like a torn cloth. His first foreign wife was Spanish (Prem Kaur), the last one a Czech (Tara Devi). In between there were numerous others of various nationalities.

Gift of a Saloon

Maharaja Jagjit Singh was very much pleased at the performance of Jarmani Dass at the Round Table Conference. He had received letters from many princes congratulating him on his choice of Jarmani Dass. On his return from London in 1930, Maharaja of Kapurthala in 1931-32 asked him what gift he could give to him for his outstanding performance. Jarmani Dass knew well how fondly the Maharaja loved his luxury Railway Coach but could not resist the temptation of asking him for it. The Maharaja was hesitant because the crown Prince Paramjeet Singh (Tikka Raja) also loved it but he would not back out from his word too. He offered to give him Rs. 2,000 in lieu of thy carriage. This was on 27th January, 1930. Jarmani Dass, apparently loved the carriage more than the money. After leaving Kapurthala, he joined service in the Patiala State. On 21st February, 1931, Diwan Jarmani Dass arranged to shift it to the Railway Shed of the then Maharaja of Patiala Bhupindar Singh. In 1939, after resigning from the Patiala State Service, the Railway Saloon was brought to Nizamuddin Railway Station. Later it was shifted to the plot of land in Nizamuddin East bought specially for this Railway saloon.

Maharaja's Spanish Wife

There was a craze among the princes for marrying white women from Europe. The pro-British Press in India exploited the weakness of the Princes and wrote derisively about Indian women. Many a Maharaja fell victim to the vile art of blackmail practised and perfected in Europe and promoted in India by the stooges of the British. Maharaja Jagjit Singh of Kapurthala was also not far behind in this race by his fellow princes. His first foreign wife was Anita Delgado or Prem Kaur. She was Spanish and was fifth in line of wives. His sixth and last wife was Tara Devi or Evgenia Grosupova of Czech origin. She was the daughter of a count. She jumped to death from the Qutab Minar in Delhi and was buried in Nicolson cemetary, Civil Lines, Delhi. He kept many mistresses for one year each on contract. The concubines were paid fabulous amount for their upkeep. After the expiry of one year the Maharaja would leave the girl in the country of her origin after giving her due compensation. There were no princes born out of such alliances except in the case of Tara Devi, a Czech girl who gave birth to prince Ajit Singh. Before accepting a mistress he used to dance with her to feel if she had warmth and kick. One of them was the Spanish dancer with whom the love affair began in 1906. The story runs like this. King Alfonso XIII of Spain invited Maharaja Jagjit Singh of Kapurthala to Spain to attend his marriage. The wedding was duly celebrated and when all was over, the Maharaja went forth to see the splendid and sparkling sights of gay Madrid. He was led to a restaurant which was famous for the beauty of its dancing girls. Here he fell in love with Anita Delgado, the dancing girl whose father sold hot potatoes on the streets of Madrid and lived on the income of his daughter. How the Maharaja proposed and married her is aptly described in the *Philadelphia Enquirer* of November 6, 1921.

"That this was no empty boast was evident when the dancing girls made their appearance, but the Maharaja was only mildly interested until there appeared on the floor a girl whose beauty outshone all the others as Venus outshines the other planets. He was immediately attracted to her and his eyes followed her every movement as she glided over the smooth floor and performed the intricate steps of a sensuous Spanish dance. Her lustrous black hair reflected the gleam of a thousand lights and her sparkling dark eyes were even brighter. Alone in the middle of the floor, she made a picture that only a Zuologa could have paralleled. The Maharaja was infatuated with this enchanting Latin beauty."

"He sought an introduction and within a few days a warm friendship developed between the wealthy, high-caste Maharaja and the lowly dancing maid. The friendship rapidly grew into love and then Maharaja was not slow in conveying his affection. The girl, strangely attracted to this man from the east returned his love. He asked her to marry him and she said that she would as soon as her father gave assent."

"So to the father went Anita Delgado, the dancing girl, but instead of offering his blessing the old man refused to listen. He was a seller of hot potatoes on the streets of his native city and the little money he made was not enough to support his family. He depended upon Anita to swell the family coffers, and if she got married his chief support would be taken from him. No, he could not hear of a marriage."

"At length the Maharaja removed the old man's objection by presenting him with a cheque for Rs. 6,000. Then there arose other objections. Did not the Maharaja have other wives, the old man asked. 'Three' he replied, but before he could explain that they would not be on the same plane as the beauteous Anita, she hastened to assure her father that it did not matter. Nothing mattered except her great love for the Maharaja."

Anita Delgado subsequently divorced the Maharaja and got an alimony of U.S. $ 5,000,000 per year plus jewels. It made the highest alimony paid in US at those times, look like peanuts. This was their style of spending money for pomp and show. India was not poor.

The Maharaja's Home Minister at that time was Sir Abdul Hamid. He was the greatest henchman of the British in India and also a bigoted Muslim. When Diwan Sahib joined the Government, a conflict between the two personalities became inevitable. The British Residents in

Kapurthala never completely trusted Diwan Sahib. They knew too well the nationalist traditions cherished by his family and of the unflinching loyalty of the family to the State and its commitment to the people. The Praja Mandal movement in the State started gathering strength. Whenever a British notable came to Kapurthala, a close watch was kept on Jarmani Dass and his brothers. Sometimes they were in their house and at others were asked to leave the State till the stay of the British VIP. Kapurthala was considered to be a den of revolutionaries because men like Bhai Parmanand and Lala Hardial used to stay in the house of the Diwan called Lal Haveli or Red Castle.

Stint as a Minister

As a Minister, Jarmani Dass toured Kapurthala State extensively and mixed up with the masses to know their problems and difficulties. He brought into existence Ayurvedic and Allopathic dispensaries in the remote areas of Patiala State where they were needed the most. He very often gave financial help to the needy from his own pocket. His greatest contributions to the State of Kapurthala was, however, the bringing into existence of a legislative assembly. He was the chief promoter of the idea of associating the people with the administration of the State. He very often recited Saadi's verse quoted in the operative part of this chapter to influence the mind of the Maharaja. Being close to the Maharaja, he succeeded in framing up his mind for this decision. This can be discovered from the Maharaja's speeches which were invariably drafted by Diwan Sahib. Even Congressmen became members of this Assembly in 1929. By this time the reactionary activities of Sir Abdul Hamid had become very abominable. The nationalist elements rose in revolt against tyranny. Every day demonstrations used to take place against him. The people ultimately succeeded in ousting him from the State.

In 1931 Maharaja Jagjit Singh gave Jarmani Dass another important assignment. He was entrusted with the work of presenting the case of ceded territories before the committee constituted to consider these cases.

He used his intimacy with the Maharaja for moulding his views on the question of increasing people's participation in the day to day affairs of the State. He did every thing in his power to expedite reforms, dilute the autocracy and promote a responsible legislature. His education and flair for writing was used by Maharaja Jagjit Singh for writing political and ceremonial addresses, it becomes clearer very soon who actually was behind the scene. For example here is a speech delivered by Maharaja Jagjit Singh on July 29, 1920 at Lancaster House (London) on the occasion of banquet given by His Majesty the King George VI of Great Britain.

"India stands on the threshold of a new era, full of beneficent possibilities, and though the Reform Act of previous year applies only to British India, I feel strongly that we, the Princes of India, governing as we do one-third of the area of that Empire, are bound to adjust the conditions in our States to changing circumstances. We must realise that we cannot stand still as detached spectators of the remarkable political progress of the world quickened by the war, but must take our part therein and show the heartiest sympathy with the spirit of the age."

"I am sure you will pardon me if I turn from the abstract to the concrete and speak of my own State. Many of you know that on the occasion of my Silver Jubilee in 1915, more than two years before the new reforms in British India were adumbrated by the Viceroy and Secretary of State, I introduced a Consultative Assembly, representing all classes and creeds, to assist in the conduct of public affairs, and more particularly in shaping progressive legislation in both social and political matters. The closer co-operation thus established between myself and my people has been attended with such happy results that very shortly I hope to introduce measures which will secure a further substantial stage of progressive evolution by bringing my people into still closer touch with me and my Government."

"For my own part, I am a firm believer in steady but cautious reform, neither lagging behind nor recklessly going ahead of the requirements of the day. There are great political tasks for us all, whether in the Indian States or in British India. I am convinced that they can only be successfully accomplished if Indians and Englishmen cordially co operate, and any racial or sectional prejudices that may exist are merged is the paramount duty of advancing the progress and prosperity of India as a whole."

The above speech by Maharaja Jagjit Singh bears the imprint of the personality of Jarmani Dass.

Freedom Movement in Kapurthala

The British dealt very strictly with the nationalist elements in India. A jail term or lathi charge in those days could mean a loss of limb or life. In the princely States, the nationalists met with far worse treatment at the hands of Rajas, Maharajas and their henchmen than in British India. People were thrown into jails without any rhyme or reason. The torture inflicted on the freedom fighters was most barbaric. Diwan Sahib's ancestral house, known as the Red Castle was favourite rendezvous of the nationalists and the revolutionaries. The activities were of course carried on in a clandestine manner. Jarmani Dass took active part in the Praja Mandal Movement in 1931. This time the local intelligence services proved too efficient to be duped by the nationalists. He became a thorn in the eye of the intelligence services.

A meeting of the political workers in the Kapurthala State was held at the house of Lala Labhu Ram Kalia in the summer of 1931 to organise a Praja Mandal. As a result of deliberations, S. Thakur Singh of Kala Sangha (latter M.L.A.) and Master Kishen Singh of Kapurthala were unanimously elected as the President and General Secretary of the Mandal respectively.

A conference of the Punjab States Praja Mandal was held at Shimla in the same year with Sardar Sardul Singh Caveeshar as its President in which the members of the Kapurthala Praja Mandal joined as delegates. The office of the reception committee was raided by the police who took possession of all the records. The same year Sir Abdul Hamid, the Prime Minister of Kapurthala went to Geneva as a delegate. Full advantage of his absence was taken by the Mandal and the workers toured all over the State carrying on agitation against the autocratic regime of the rulers. Before proceeding to Geneva Sir Abdul Hamid had manipulated that some of his trusted friends, both Muslims and non-Muslims should join the Praja Mandal in order to work as spies as also to torpedo the movement. But unfortunately for him, the leaders of the Praja Mandal movement proved too clear to be duped and used their presence as means of promoting the cause of the Mandal. On his return from Geneva the Chief Minister was surprised to discover things going quite contrary to his expectations and in a fit of rage directed all his men to leave the Mandal *en bloc* which they did. But the movement went on getting momentum and the whole State was astir with political awareness.

When Mahatma Gandhi came back from London after attending the Round Table Conference in 1932, he launched the Satyagraha movement against the foreign rule on a countrywide scale. Instructions were received from the All India States Peoples' Conference to suspend the activities of the Mandal, and to concentrate on the Satyagraha Movement. Accordingly, a batch of 11 volunteers from village Kala Sangha was sent to Lahore to offer Satyagraha. The Trio, viz.

Hazara Singh, Chanan Singh and Ujaghar Singh broke the statue of Lord Lawrence at the Mall Road and courted arrest. Lord Lawrence was depicted as holding a pen in one hand and a sword in the other. They were sentenced to two years rigorous imprisonment each with fine. But Sir Hamid was terrified at this act by men from his State. He thought the British masters might force him to resign from the job. He, there, ordered for the repairs of the statue at the cost of the State. As a result, the property of the four brave men was put on auction but to the great chagrin of the Prime Minister, nobody came forward to buy. He was contemplating some other drastic measures to make his order effective when *The Tribune* came to the rescue of these gallant patriots and in an editorial note questioned the propriety of the order when the case was yet subjudice and no judgement had been pronounced. This note had the desired effect and the Maharaja issued orders withdrawing the auction proceedings. The suffering of these selfless patriots was great but washed away a standing disgrace. The white masters were forced to change the inscription beneath the statue. The inscription was: "Will you be ruled by sword or by pen?" It was changed to "I will serve thee with pen and sword". In 1934 All India States People Conference appointed an enquiry committee to go into the allegations against the late Maharaja of Patiala in which Master Tara Singh and Master Kishen Singh from Kapurthala and Sohan Singh Gorh from Punjab were called to assist in the conduction of the inquiry.

The Struggle continued for several years and the climax

reached in 1943 during the Prime Ministership of K.B. Mian Abdul Aziz who, in order to punish the workers, charged them with being in conspiracy with the Germans. The agitators were hauled up one morning in 1943 from all parts of the State. Master Kishan Singh and Giani Harcharan Singh were prosecuted for waging war against his Majesty the King of Great Britain and Emperor of India and they were imprisoned for a long term.

Tour of Japan

As has been stated earlier, when Jarmani Dass went from one country to another he keenly observed men, women, their tradition, culture, etc. He has left for the posterity elaborate sketches of the emperors, generals and dictators that he met. His observations are most genuine. If needed, Jarmani Dass does not even spare himself. With a few deft touches he transports the reader to the presence of the person he describes. Here is an interesting account of Japan in the lucid language of Jarmani Dass:

"I have been to Japan seven times but always I recollect my first visit to that fascinating country geographically surnamed as 'Land of the Rising Sun'. 40 years ago, when I met the Emperor who is reigning for the last 45 years. His name Hirohito means exalted. When a Japanese Emperor begins his reign he is given another name and when he dies he is known by the adopted name. Hirohito's reign is called 'Show' (Radiant Peace) and when he dies he will be known as Emperor Showa."

"Emperor Hirohito was always referred to by his subjects as Teishi-Sama (Son of Heaven). The Emperors in Japan are never crowned but accede to the Crown. As he himself is a God, he only prays to his ancestors. I was received by the Emperor in a small round room at the Palace in Tokyo which was well furnished with glittering ceiling and artistic old Japanese paintings and beautiful white Chrysanthemum flowers. The Emperor was in a military uniform. Conversation took place between the Emperor and myself standing and later on in the evening I was entertained to a large garden party called 'Chrysanthemum Festival', to celebrate the Chrysanthemum season where five to six thousand guests assembled and all the noble Japanese gentlemen and diplomats were in frock suits with top hats just like in London at the Buckingham Palace where the ladies were dressed like Westerners in the office and at home like their nationals in Kimonos. I observed at this garden party that refreshment included a gag of sweets at each table for each guest who was supposed to take back these gifts of sweets from the Palace for distribution to their families as well as their domestic servants who in turn will distribute them to their own families and so forth."

In Ethiopia – The Land of Solomon and Sheba

Jarmani Dass met Emperor Haile Selassie of Ethiopia at its capital Addis Ababa. The Emperor developed a strong liking for him and bestowed on him the highest honour of his empire. He has left a vivid account of his audience with the Emperor.

"The Emperor sits in the medieval splendour of his palace in Addis Ababa with his pet lion Tojo at his side and a retinue of courtiers called Rases around him. He is respected by the Muslim Arab World in spite of his being a Christian. For the races of noblemen are very much a law into themselves and it is their free spending, lose-living which have stirred up so much of the opposition to the Emperor that is showing itself today in student riots, savage anti-Emperor pamphlets and bomb attacks. Haile Salessie has tried but failed to control these rowdy nobles."

"He still studies long into the night to see he can find new ways of giving his people what they want but perhaps the difficulty is that nobody will tell him just what it is they want."

"Until a few years back the people had so much respect for the Emperor that they had to crawl on stomach when they approached him. Haile Sellassie has abolished this custom but still like in the time of the Maharajas of India and the Sultan of Morocco or the Sultan of Turkey, visitors must leave his presence backward in order not to turn the back to the Emperor."

In America

Maharaja Jagjit Singh was the accredited representative of the Indian princes to the League of Nations, Geneva. On his return from Geneva, he halted for three months at Paris his most favourite city and from there he went to the U.S. to meet

President Herbert Hoover. This was his fourth visit to the U.S. He was accompanied by Diwan Jarmani Dass, Diwan Mohabbat Rai, three attendants and forty pieces of luggage. The Press in Washington gave screamers like "fabulously rich Indian Prince arrives in State", "Indian Maharaja plans talk with Hoover" etc. As usual he talked of his jewels, palaces, parties and splendour. Some of the statements he made include the following:

"To value my jewels is difficult. For example, two years ago I purchased some beautiful emeralds in Paris for my turban, but no value can be placed upon them. The value of my jewels is in their historical importance and in the beauty of the stone."

"And there is my own palace in Kapurthala – the finest palace in the whole of India. Twenty years ago, I brought the best architects from Europe to build it for me, after the Louis XVI style. It is not the largest, but the most beautiful."

"Oh, yes – almost forgot," he said. "I celebrated my golden jubilee two years ago in my palace – fifty years since my accession to my father's throne in 1877, when I was but five years old. It was the greatest celebration in the history of India."

While making a frank admission of the splendour of his golden jubilee, Maharaja Jagjit Singh recalled the "house party" he once hosted for 2000 guests which cost him a rare fortune. At that time he had invited the late Elbert H. Cary of the United States Steel Corporation of India to attend his fiftieth birthday party which as, he had promised, turned out to be the most dazzling spectacle Occidental eyes had ever feasted upon.

Another newspaperman Mr. T. H. K. Rezmile also interviewed the Maharaja. His report published in the papers the next day is as follows :

"Their Highness the Indian ruling Princes are now fully in sympathy with the aspirations of Indian people for the establishment of democratic and responsible institutions of governments of India," said the Maharaja's military secretary and authorised spokesman Sardar Jarmani Dass, at the Savoy-Plaza yesterday, after I had made my bow to His Highness, who intently listened. "The British Government has long been in consultation with the Princes on the subject of the granting of self-government to British India and what will inevitably follow the introduction of democratic system of rule in the Indian States; and the enlightened and gracious Highnesses, through their chamber at Delhi, have assured the Government of His Britannic Majesty of their willingness to co-operate in whatever measures the paramount power decides to take in the matter."

After Washington, the party visited Detroit as guests of Mr. Ford and later visited Niaghara Falls, Philadelphia, Chicago and several other cities. All travel arrangements were made by Diwan Jarmani Dass.

L' Affair Pellegrino

Maharaja Jagjit Singh used to remain absent from his State

for pretty long periods, sometimes as long as ten months in a year. He had weakness for beautiful European women. Every year he used to visit Europe, marry a beauty, bring her to India and leave her the next year as a worn cloth. A vivid description of the Maharaja's dalliance is given by Diwan Sahib in his celebrated books *Maharaja* and *Maharani.* A czech wife who was given the name Tara Devi committed suicide by jumping from Qutab Minar. She had been teased by one Mathura Das, the then Private Secretary to His Highness. Madam Pellegrino of Champs Elysee was the bewitching beauty of Paris. Sometime during 1930 Maharaja Jagjit Singh happened to have a rendezvous with her on a sea-side resorts in bikinis. He had heard of her beauty and grace earlier but had not met her. It was a case of love at first sight. He admitted to his courtiers that an electric shock had reverberated through his body on seeing her. She was an intelligent, majestic looking, tall buxom lady with curvaceous figure. She was also comely, vivacious, mixing and adventurous type. The Maharaja used all the allurements at his command to project himself as an "eligible" person and the two became friends. Soon she started sharing the bed with Maharaja. Pellegrino first lived with him at Paris and then came to live with him, like numerous other beauties from Europe before her, at Kapurthala. As she was a mistress and not a Maharani, she enjoyed comparative freedom. Lahore was at that time the cultural centre of Punjab. She expressed a desire to go to Lahore regularly for dancing and to the beauticians. She also wanted to go to hill stations for trekking and enjoying nature. She asked the Maharaja to send Jarmani with her to serve as her partner for dancing at Lahore and other places. The Maharaja granted her request without hesitation. Pellegrino also could not think of a better person than Jarmani Dass because he had attained perfection in Western dances. Pellegrino soon became an admirer of Jarmani. Sir Abdul Hamid was watching the romantic development very carefully. When the Maharaja left for Paris in the company of Pellegrino, Sir Abdul Hamid inducted four of his trusted spies in the Maharaja's party. One of the spies was Khushal Singh who had masterminded many a conspiracies earlier at the behest of Sir Abdul Hamid. Now his duty was to "expose" Jarmani Dass even if he had to concoct a cock and bull story against him. One day Pellegrino rang up Jarmani Dass. The telephone was intercepted and the romantic conversation was heard by the Maharaja. On the other side Sir Abdul Hamid was sending letters to the Maharaja against the Diwan depicting him as a person who indulged in anti-State activities. As the Maharaja confronted Jarmani Dass with these letters, he got provoked and resigned there and then from the Maharaja's service. Jarmani Dass thought himself to be an indispensable person to the Maharaja and expected the Maharaja to reject his letter of resignation, but it was not to be so.

Rasputin in Maharaja's Court

The Maharaja dismissed Jarmani Dass. He was ordered to sail to India by the first available P&O Liner. He was also debarred from entering the Kapurthala State. The ban was later modified and he was allowed to enter the state for a period not exceeding four days on the occasion of some bereavement in the family. Pellegrino felt very sorry at this development which had taken place entirely because of her inadvertence. She cut off her relation with the Maharaja and married Henry Ford of America. Henry Ford also left a huge fortune for her. Later on when asked how much wealth she had got she explained she did not know herself. The friendship of Jarmani Dass with Pellegrino proved very lasting. As late as in 1957 she wrote to him as his most dependable friend eager to do anything at his bidding. She married one rich photographer and was known as Mme Germaine De Maria. She lived at 68 Av. Des Champs-Elysee, Paris. Her son Francois is a leading businessman of France. She owns a number of Cinema houses in France. When Mrs. Sushila Dass visited France in 1961 she met Mme Pellegrino.

On his return to India, Bibi Kam Kandla, the first wife of Jarmani Dass refused to join him in this period of adversity. His brother Diwan Wilaiti Ram suffered a heart attack on learning of his resignation. His cousin brother Lala Baldev Dass gave him lot of solace during this period. He settled for sometime at Palampur.

The Two Round Table Conferences : 1930 & 1931

The Round Table Conference is an important landmark in

the history of freedom movement in India. It was summoned by the British Government after the nationalist leaders had repudiated the recommendations of the Simon Commission. The purpose of the Conference was to arrive at a consensus for reforming the Indian Constitution. There were 16 representatives of the political parties, 16 delegates from the Indian States and 57 delegates from British India including some prominent Indian personalities like Sir Tej Bahadur Sapru, Mr. Srinivasa Sastri, Mr. C. Y. Chintamoni, Dr. B. R. Ambedkar and Sir Mohd. Shafi. Representatives of Indian womanhood also took part in it, such as Mrs. Sarojini Naidu, who after Independence became the first women Governor of U.P. It was a rare honour to attend this conference. The name of Diwan Jarmani Dass as an Adviser was approved by none else than the British Prime Minister Mr. Ramsay MacDonald who also happened to be his personal friend.

Round Table Conference, 1930 : First Session

The First Round Table Conference took place at 12 noon on Wednesday, the 12th of November, 1930 at Royal Gallery, House of Lords. The session lasted up to 19 January 1931. It was also attended by Jarmani Dass as an Adviser to the Princes' delegation. He played a very pivotal role in the first and the second Round Table Conferences. He has left behind for posterity the vivid details of this conference. The newspaper cuttings of that year show how precise and penetrating his observations proved 40 years later. The delegates are shown in the photographs dressed in all their finery. Many of the British officers and politicians were personally known to Diwan Sahib. The Princes approached him for getting invitations for them to see the races in the Royal Box at Ascot. Sir Clive Wigram used to agree to Diwan Sahib's request. He also got them invitations from the Royal Chamberlain for dinner at the Buckingham Palace. The Princes were amazed when the Prime Minister, Mr. Ramsay MacDonald invited him to dine at 10 Downing Street. He also knew all the Princes and the nationalist leaders very intimately. This placed him in a position of advantage. Lord Sankey, who presided over the Federal Structure Committee, was his chum. This committee was the most important of all the committees. Protocol was strictly adhered to. The ceremonial part of the conference was well rehearsed. Begum Shah Nawaz from Punjab was the most glamorous lady among the delegates. Sir Khizer Hayat came dressed in Shalwar-Achkan with a long tuft of his turban fluttering in the air. Jarmani Dass was ever ready to extend financial assistance and moral support to every one who approached him for it. Even without taking part in debates he helped in determining attitudes and final shaping of policies.

In the words of Maharaja Bhupinder Singh of Patiala, he worked in a remarkably able manner winning applause from all the delegates. Long after the conference he continued to receive letters of thanks from the delegates and the officials. An extract from his observations is given below:

"The opening of the Round Table Conference took place in the Royal Gallery of the House of Lords on Wednesday,

12th November 1930, with stately splendour for the first time, the King of Great Britain presided over this and called upon the delegates of the conference to deal with the tremendous problem of India's future Constitution. There were 86 delegates in all – 16 from the Indian States, 57 representing British India and 13 from political parties. The Rt. Hon'ble J. Ramsay MacDonald, Prime Minister of England, the ruling Princes of India and their ministers, sat on the right of the throne and the Secretary of State Hon'ble Sir Wedgewood Benn and the other British delegates sat on the left and the British Indian leaders were seated at the front. In opening the Conference, His Majesty the Emperor said:

"It gives me most satisfaction to welcome to the capital of my empire, representatives of other parties composing the Parliament in whose precincts we are assembled."

In the end the King said:

"May your discussion pave the way to ensure achievement of this end and may your name go down in history as those of the men who served India, whose endeavour advanced the happiness and prosperity of all my beloved people. I pray that providence may grant you a bounteous measure of wisdom, patience and goodwill."

It was a gorgeous sight to see the King, his Ministers, the delegates from India assembled in the magnificent gallery of the House of Lords.

The speech of His Majesty was followed by that of the Prime Minister Ramsay MacDonald of England, Maharaja

Sayaji Rao Gaekwad of Baroda, Maharaja Hari Singh of Kashmir, Mr. M.A. Jinnah and others. The Maharaja of Baroda spoke of Queen Victoria's famous proclamation namely, "India's prosperity will be our strength and their contentment our security, in their gratitude our best reward". The best speech on the opening day was that of Mr. M.A. Jinnah who said in a very powerful and clear tone:

"I call upon all the premiers and representatives of the dominions who are here to witness the birth of a new dominion of the British Commonwealth."

The Congress Party had refused invitation to attend the Conference. After the King left the Royal Gallery, Maharaja Bhupinder Singh, the Chancellor of the Chamber of Princes proposed in a short speech that Mr. MacDonald, the Prime Minister of Great Britain should preside over the Conference. Later on, many Committees were formed but the most important Committee was the Federal Structure Committee of which Lord Sankey, Chancellor of the Exchequer, was elected as President. It is in this Committee that the Indian Princes, the British delegates and the representatives of British India aired their political views.

The Congress had refused to attend the first session of the Round Table Conference because its avowed object fell short of its demand. It had declared complete independence as its goal on the banks of Ravi at Lahore in 1929. It had launched the Gandhi-Irwin Pact. The Congress decided to join the second session of the Round Table Conference and elected Mahatma Gandhi as its sole representative.

Round Table Conference, 1931 : Second Session

The Second Round Table Conference took place in 1931. Its session lasted from 7 September to 1 December 1931. Diwan Jarmani Dass attended it as a substitute delegate in place of Maharaja Jagjit Singh. It as was attended by Mahatma Gandhi and many other nationalist leaders like Mrs. Sarojini Naidu, Pandit Madan Mohan Malaviya, etc. Shri M.R. Jayakar, a leading Advocate of India and a very close friend of Diwan Jarmani Dass, as well as the Maharaja of Baroda, Bikaner and Patiala, Sir Tej Bahadur Sapru, another close friend of Diwan Jarmani Dass, and Mohammed Ali Jinnah also attended the Second Round Table Conference. He spent a good deal of time discussing various matters with Jarmani Dass whom he respected very much for his brilliance. As in the first conference, he was all pervasive in the Second Conference. Luckily for the historians, he has left very interesting notes on this momentous Conference. It is a sheer delight to read them. No detail missed his keen observation. Take for example Mahatma Gandhi's loin-cloth and the impasse it created. Mahatma Gandhi insisted on attending all the functions in his usual dress i.e. in the loin-cloth. This created a ticklish situation well described by Diwan Jarmani Dass below:

"The Second Round Table Conference was called in 1931 in which Mahatma Gandhi, Mrs. Sarojini Naidu, Pandit Madan Mohan Malaviya and other eminent leaders, such as Sir Tej Bahadur Sapru, Rt. Hon'ble Mr. M.R. Jayakar, the Maharajas of Baroda, Bikaner, Patiala and others participated. The speeches of Mahatma Gandhi were heard most attentively. After his short and excited conversation with the King of England at a reception at the Buckingham Palace, he made his historic speech when he said, referring to a talk he had with an English gentleman: 'My children in India treat British bombs and bullets as mere crackers.' Here I would like to narrate how Mahatma Gandhi mentioned bombs and crackers at the Federal Structure Committee. One day all the delegates and advisors from India to the Round Table Conference were invited to the Buckingham Palace by the King, the Emperor of India for an afternoon reception and there was a lot of fuss regarding the dress which Mahatma Gandhi should wear while attending the function. At the left hand side of the invitation card was marked 'Morning Dress' which meant that the Indian guests should wear national dress, and morning suit or frock coat with top hat was the dress prescribed for the Europeans. Mahatma Gandhi would not attend the reception in any dress other than what most of the poor Indians wore that is a loin cloth or Langoti. There was a grave impasse when Mahatma Gandhi declared his intention. The King and Queen strongly resented it. The Secretary of State for India wired to the Earl of Willingdon, Viceroy of India, for his advice in the matter. The Viceroy informed the Secretary of State that there would be great resentment in India if Mahatma Gandhi was not allowed to attend this reception at the Buckingham Palace due to proper regulation. So the King and Queen were forced against their wishes to have Mahatma Gandhi in his usual dress at the reception. I was also invited to this function as a delegate from India and I stood and talked in the portico with Mahatma Gandhi who was in this dress with a white shawl over his shoulders and looked like a prophet. He was accompanied by Mrs. Sarojini Naidu along with all the delegates and advisors from India, Princes, Dukes and members of the aristocracy of England with their consorts gorgeously dressed and the Prime Minister and Ministers of the Government of Great Britain and officers of the Political Department, high ranking officers of the Army. The Navy and the Air Force were present at this function. The total number of guests on this occasion was less than 2000. A few yards from the portico where Mahatma Gandhi stood, the King and the Queen received their guests inside the magnificent and spacious audience hall at the Buckingham Palace. The guests were presented by Lord Chamberlain to the King and the Queen, announcing their names and the King brought his hand forward and shook the hand of each guest who passed on to the Queen who also shook hands with them. Mahatma Gandhi was the last guest to enter the drawing room. I remember that when Mahatma Gandhi entered the room his name was not announced. Though the King shook hands with him, the Queen withdrew her hand and Mahatma Gandhi was ushered into the centre of the Hall away from the other guests by an enquiry-in-waiting. It was there that the King met him and had a talk with him which was later narrated to me by Mrs. Sarojini Naidu who was my personal friend of long standing. The eyes of all guests were focussed on the centre where the King and Mahatma Gandhi were standing. The King looked excited and angry. It was a unique and unforgettable sight to see the King in frock coat with checkered trousers, talking to Mahatma Gandhi dressed in loin-cloth. The King told Mahatma Gandhi:

"You were a friend of the British in Africa and I do not understand how now you turned against me and the British Government and I warn you if you create disturbance in India and do not co-operate with my Government I have my army there, which will blow up all agitators and conspirators."

The Mahatma kept quiet and the King walked away to talk to other guests. To this speech of the King, Gandhi replied, "My children in India will treat your bombs and bullets as crackers."

How He Torpedoed a Plan

During the entire Round Table Conference, the Indian Princes played second fiddle to the British bureaucrats and politicians. Their sole aim was to checkmate the nationalist movement. They wanted the conference to fail. The second alternative before them was to control the entire country through a constitution that gave them numerical majority. The most dangerous suggestion was made by the Maharaja of Dholpur. He wanted a Confederation of Indian States which could negotiate for a coalition government with the elected representatives from British India. This was a very dangerous idea. If the idea had caught wings, things would have become very difficult for the nationalists at a later stage. The pro-British Princes would have become all powerful for all time to come. The integration of States achieved by Sardar Patel after 1947 would have taken much more time and a heavy price would have been paid for it. The farsighted Diwan Jarmani Dass had the uncanny sense to think of the future. So with the help of his friends Sir Tej Bahadur Sapru and Rt. Hon'ble M.R. Jayakar he scuttled the nefarious plan of the Princes through his soft tongue and persuasive manners.

Hostility of the Princes

The Princes at the Conference did not hide their hostility to the freedom movement and their rove for the British rule. They did not want India to be free. They thought that would put an end to their autocratic rule in their States. In their private circles they poured scorn over Mahatma Gandhi. They referred to him as Maha Tuma (most greedy). For this reason, Jarmani Dass nursed deep hatred for the Princes. It was at this time and for this reason that the seeds of hatred for the Princes were sown in his mind. He had an encounter with M.A Jinnah and some British politicians at the conference which he described with a penetrating insight:

"Mahatma Gandhi was not much liked by the British politicians, particularly officials in the Indian Office. I was sitting one morning in the gallery of St. James' Palace where the meetings of Federal Structure Committee were held and was talking to Mr. P. Patrick, Secretary of State for India when suddenly Mahatma Gandhi passed by us to attend a meeting of the Federal Structure Committee. I stood up and bowed to him and Mr. Patrick remained sitting and told me afterwards that Mahatma Gandhi was a self-centred man and was very egoistic but I differed with his opinion on Gandhi and explained to him that Mahatma Gandhi was quite a different and venerable personality. He obviously disagreed. I told him that as Mahatma Gandhi did not talk much, he gave a wrong impression about himself. Another time, I was sitting on the same sofa with M.A. Jinnah. He was in most dejected mood and never cared for the Federation nor did he consider Congress leaders as his friends. He told me that under the leadership of the then Congress leaders, it was not possible for him to find out any formula by which the Congress, Muslim League and other parties could get together. I differed with him and told him that we should try to find out a via media. Then he retorted: "If I were dealing with people like you, Jarmani, I would be able to come to some arrangement about the future of the country but when I am dealing with men like Sardar Vallabhbhai Patel I have no chances of finding a common political formula."

After his return from London, Diwan Jarmani Dass was flooded with letters from eminent leaders of public opinion, intellectuals and princes complementing him for the brilliant role he had played at the Conference. Letters were received by Maharaja Jagjit Singh complementing him for sparing the services of his minister. One such letter from Maharaja

Bhupinder Singh of Patiala is reproduced in the last chapter of this book.

K.N. Haksar, Director, Special Organisation of the Chamber of Princes wrote to Maharaja Jagjit Singh on 22 January, 1932, from Savoy Hotels, London eulogizing the services of Sardar Jarmani Dass. To quote:

"He proved an invaluable liaison between us of the Indian States Delegation and Government circles on the one hand and British leaders on the other. He works unostentatiously behind the scenes. He combines great personal charm of manner with a natural capacity for diplomatic conversation."

Sir Tej Bahadur Sapru wrote to Maharaja Bhupinder Singh after the Conference about the fine and effective speech Diwan Sahib made at the Conference. In this letter he spoke very highly of him. Maharaja Bhupinder Singh himself wrote to thank him for the services he rendered to the State delegation. The Jam Sahib of Nawanaghar also praised him for his role in the Conference.

It was not all work only at the Round Table Conference. The delegates had happy interludes as well. But for the observant eye and facile pen of Jarmani Dass, these sidelights would have remained unknown to posterity. One such interlude as described by Dajon mentioned below:

"Members of the Round Table Conference had a pleasant interlude in their strenuous labours when they watched an exhibition of dances at Dorchester House, organised by the Maharani of Baroda for Charity. A glittering array of

Indian Princes and other notables were present, and they obviously keenly appreciated the delightful programme, notably the performance of "Menaka" (Mrs. Sokhey). To the accompaniment of violin, piano and drum she interpreted India according to the results of her studies of old Indian sculpture and painting. One enthusiast described her as a brown flame', a flame against black velvet, a trifle of brown dressing, her body sang songs, made dread despair and wild triumph."

"Certainly she displayed real feeling, rhythm in blithe and graceful movement, with her beautiful arms Alung upward, her red lips, parted in a smile, her lustrous eyes flashing and her jet black hair accentuating the brown of the face and shoulder in a darkened room of gold and white.

A famous Hungarian caricaturist Emery Kelen had also come to London to cover the round table conferences of 1930 in his own way. Through the influence of Diwan Jarmani Das he managed to draw the caricatures of the eminent Indian Maharajas at the Conference. In his lifetime the caricaturist had never come across such a contrast in personalities, types, gait and costume. Many of these caricatures were published in the newspapers of the time. All the Maharaja who attended were given a printed copy of his sketches.

Mr. Kelen reveals in his drawings a power of seizing and ascending the salient feature of each sitter which is the very essence of caricature.

"If this power is used with the spice of malice, the

caricature is apt to become offensive; but there is not an atom of malice in Mr. Kelen's good-natured fur. The best proof is the readiness shown by the Indian Princes to order, not a single copy, but a whole series of this album, which will be treasured as much for its artistry as for its importance as an historical document."

"Mr. Kelen's pictorial records of the outward traits of the politicians engaged in international conferences have found a place in the archives of every foreign ministry and embassy in Europe."

Diwan Jarmani Dass had a very large circle of friends in London. Many Indians settled in U.K. and British business firms were eager to establish friendly links with him. The occasion of the Round Table Conference therefore proved a boon to all such people who were eager to renew their friendship with him. Many Princes took advantage of his contacts and extended their own circle. He received an invitation from the King Emperor and the Queen Empress. The Rt. Honourable, J. Ramsay MacDonald invited him for dinner. Others to invite him were Earl of Stradbroke, Lord Pinhy, Mrs. Pardhy, Mrs. Lloyd Baxendale, The Marquess of Linlithgow, Lady Maud Hoare, Mrs. Meyer Sasoon, Lady Isa Bella Howard, the Dowager Marchioness of Dufferin and Ava, Lady Seton, Lady Halland, Lady Wheller, Sir Willian Vincent, the Lord Chancellor and Mrs. Sanky, the Lord President of the Conncila and Lady Parmoor, Viscountess Astar, Lady Pentland and Miss Valeree Wallace on behalf of British Federation of University Women. There was a dinner with the Editor of The *spectator* The prominent Indians who invited him for dinner were Nawab Sir Mohammed Akbar Hydari, Moulvi Farzand Ali Imam of the London Mosque, Dr. I.G. De Silva; Nawab Mohd. Jamshed Ali, Khan, Lady Amin Jung, Mrs. Subbarayan, Begum Shah Nawaz, Mrs. M.C. Ghose and Mrs. R.S. Mehra. There were invitations from firms like Humber & Hillman.

Minister in Patiala, 1933-1939

"The well-being of a people is like a tree; agriculture is its roots, manufacture and commerce are its branches and its life; if the root is injured the leaves fall, the branches break away and the tree dies."

A Chinese Adage

The State of Patiala came into existence in 1751. Ahmed Shah Abdali had invaded India several times and whenever he returned to Afghanistan, his camels groaned under the weight of loot which was mainly gold. He also used to take back home a larger number of men and women as slaves. He obviously needed help of the local chieftains on his return journeys after the predatory invasions. Pleased at the support given to him by Baba Ala Singh, the founder of Patiala, he conferred upon him the title of Raja. His grandson Amar Singh got the title of Maharaja from Abdali when he came again to invade the country. From 1809 onwards the State of Patiala came under the protection of the British. Although Sikh State, the Maharaja preferred the British to Maharaja Ranjit Singh. Once again during the "Mutiny" the House of Patiala got an opportunity to demonstrate its loyalty to the British. For these services (betrayals of freedom) the Maharaja was given a territory yielding a revenue of two lakhs. When Jarmani Dass joined the service of the state, the ruler was Maharaja Bhupinder Singh. The tales of his "adventure" were all well known. The State had a nursery of virgins where young girls were reared till maturity and then deflowered by the cohorts of the Maharaja. His fondness wine and women was well-known. He was however, a man of considerable personality, a born leader and a great philanthropist. He was a scholar of Vedanta and philosophy. He was a great cricketer and a patron of sportsmen. It may surprise many that the greatest beneficiaries of his philanthropy were the Pandits of Banaras (Varanasi). He had an uncanny sense of selecting the right person for the right job. He was strongly committed to the traditions of the State. The women in the families of the ministers and other high officials of the State were expected to observe strict purdah. During marriages and other functions all had to wear a set dress comprising saffron, ochre-coloured robes. In spite of his follies and foibles he was loved by his people because he was a person of wisdom and generosity.

After the First and Second Round Table Conferences in London in 1930 and 1931, Diwan Jarmani Dass attended the sessions of the League of Nations at Geneva in 1932. He was adviser to the Indian Chamber of Princes Delegation to the first Conference and a substitute delegate to the second one. His performance at the Round Table Conference was appreciated by one and all in India, particularly, Mahatma Gandhi, Father of the Nation. Maharaja Bhupinder Singh, therefore, was keen to get him in his service. He offered ministership to Diwan Jarmani Dass which he accepted. He felt happy that he was available for employment under him. He believed the loss of Kapurthala was the gain of Patiala. On his return from Europe after relinquishing his job with the Maharaja of Kapurthala, he preferred to relax at Palampur, from where he proceeded to Patiala to take up his new assessment. The news of his appointment spread quickly and he was flooded with letters congratulating him on getting this appointment. Among those who wrote to him on the occasion were the ruling princes, heir-apparents, Deans and eminent Public figures.

As a Minister in Patiala, he was made in-charge of the Departments of Commerce, Industry, Agriculture, Animal Husbandry, Rural Development, Forests, Garages, Health, Photography and Aviation. He was also made Chairman of the City Improvement Board. He was also made guardian of the Maharaja's children. In Patiala it was obligatory for everyone in service to wear a turban. The women were expected to observe strict purdah. This was made clear to him by His Highness Maharaja Bhupinder Singh. He agreed to his wishes which are symbols of India's heritage. Diwan

Jarmani Dass who had always been an orthodox person, complied most readily.

As a minister in the Patiala State Services he did a lot of constructive and social work which bears a testimony of his love for the common man. For this, he is still remembered in Patiala. He used his administrative experience and contacts in India and abroad for the benefit of the State. He used to tour the State extensively by car and or on horseback for streamlining the administration of the departments under him. He raised the level of their efficiency and thus boosted the revenues of the State. He generated lot of employment by starting industrial enterprises such as Bhupindra Cement Works at Surajpur which is situated on way to Shimla near Pinjore gardens. For the first time in India, ropeways were installed for this factory.

He brought about vast improvements in Horticulture Department. New orchards were laid in accordance with the recommendations of Prof. R.W. Hodgson of the University of California who came to Patiala on the invitation of Diwan Jarmani Dass. He toured Kulu and Kashmir to study if fruits grown there could also be grown in Patiala. He improved the dairy farms and streamlined the Agriculture Department. He regularly organized cattlefarms, to increase the revenue of the State, prepared a Working Plan for the settlement of forests in the hill territory of the State such as Pinjore, Kandaghat. He protected them from poachers and encouraged afforestation – an honest environmentalist indeed.

He reorganized the Reception and Household Department under his control. The Rest Homes were provided with sanitary fittings.

In the period of one and a half year he brought about a saving of rupees three lakhs in the budget of the departments under his control. In those days this was quite a substantial amount.

He worked for the construction of the stadium and other buildings. He brought about considerable economy in the building activity.

He formulated rules and regulations to govern the daily duties of the personal staff. With a strong and stem hand he eliminated indiscipline.

Ultra-modern guest house with modern sanitary fittings at vintage points, were built all over the state.

He formulated rules for the entertainment of guests. Previously there were no rules or norms of any kind and everything depended on the whims of the officers. He increased the efficiency of all the departments under his control.

He took care of the health of the Maharaja in 1935 in Europe where he developed high blood pressure, and later in India. Many times the Maharaja thanked him for his honest and bold advice. He appointed Prof. Abrami, the best physician of Europe as the Maharaja's Physician. He was paid rupees one lakh per month free of income tax besides other facilities including boarding, lodging, hard drinks and transport.

He created agricultural boards and reformed the Agriculture Department and Sanitation Department.

He beautified the town through the Improvement Trust Board.

He was Chairman of this Board. He resigned from this Board on November 6, 1939.

As in-charge of the Department of Agriculture, he started many dairy farms on modern lines. He attended the All India Conferences on Agriculture and Cattle which were presided over by the Viceroy.

He visited countries like Argentina, France and the USA to study the latest techniques of agriculture and put them to practice back home at Patiala.

He set-up an X-Ray institution in Patiala under the charge of Dr. Pulitzer and opened many Ayurvedic dispensaries in the countryside.

He gave a fillip to agriculture and horticulture in the State by arranging loans and high quality seeds for the farmers. Visits were arranged for horticultural experts from California, such as Professor Hodgson.

Prof. Hodgson was entrusted with the job of surveying and studying the meteorology, climatology of the orchards and lush green gardens of Kulu and Kashmir so that the same could be developed in the foothills of Patiala State like Chail, Kandaghat, Kufri, Pinjore, etc.

He built many new buildings and roads which now form a part of modern Patiala.

He organised agricultural exhibitions, cattle fairs. He improved the sanitary conditions of villages and towns. He encouraged cooperative systems and arranged loans for farmers.

The State witnessed torrential rains in 1935 which caused widespread damage, suffering and devastation. A Central Relief Committee was formed under the Chairmanship of Nawab Sir Liaqat Hayat Khan. The Maharaja also took keen interest in the relief operations. Diwan Jarmani Dass worked day and night to give solace to the poor people of the State. He was the moving spirit of the Relief Committee. The Maharaja recorded and conveyed his appreciation to him through his Prime Minister.

For six years he was a member of the Cabinet and for one and half year, Military Secretary. In this capacity he did his best to serve the State. When he resigned in 1939, his services to the State were appreciated by Maharaja Yaduvinder Singh in the State gazette.

Patiala House

The Patiala House in Delhi which now houses the Delhi High Court at Tilak Marg was built during Diwan Jarmani Dass's time. When New Delhi was being built, plots of land were offered to the princes and Diwans for constructing their state Houses in the imperial Capital. When a similar plot was given to Patiala State some officials over there hesitated to spend State money on building in Delhi. Diwan Sahib put his weight on the side of constructing a palatial building to be named Patiala House. Sardar Narain Singh and his partner Bawa Harkishan Dass, one of the reputed builders at New Delhi approached Diwan Sahib for the building contract and offered him the princely sum of Rs. 2,000 for giving them the said contract. Diwan Sahib angrily turned down the offer of money although Sardar Narain Singh got the contract. Ever since then Sardar Narain Singh and Bawa Harkishan Dass became great admirers of Diwan Sahib.

Pleased by his deeds, Maharaja Bhupinder Singh conferred upon him the title of Diwan. He was made in charge of 600 palace children and of about 326 Ranis and Maharanis. He got the portfolio in health and aviation. He maintained strict discipline in the household. Even the heir-apparent Yaduvinder Singh could not straightway go and see his father, Bhupinder Singh, the Maharaja. He had to seek Diwan Sahib's permission for the same. It was as a result of this discipline that the Prince grew up into a fine young man free from the vices from which his father and the aristocracy suffered. He learnt the work of each department of the Government so much so that he was made to work even as a Patwari. Later on when he took over the administration one could befool him because of his mastery over the details. Maharaja Bhupinder Singh died at a young age owing to blood pressure. When Yaduvinder ascended the throne he gave lot of importance to Jarmani Dass. Very often he addressed him as uncle and raised his status to Military Secretary. However, in spite of the young Maharaja's regards for him, he had to leave the service of the State as a disillusioned man.

A Plan for Dumas

Maharaja Bhupinder Singh of Patiala knew well of Diwan Jarmani Dass ability to get things done at the level of the Viceroy's Executive Council. Maharaja Bhupinder Singh once approached Jarmani to procure his secret file from Vice Regal Lodge (now Rashtrapati Bhawan). Diwan Jarmani Dass managed to get it through R.B. Gopal Das, the then Superintendent C.I.D. His contacts with the ruling elite were also well-known to the princes. Many British civil servants were known to him personally since his college days. The ruling princes, therefore, approached him for advice and help frequently. His familiarity with tourist spots of the world was also well-known. The ruler of Sachin, a small State in the South approached him to plan for him a casino at Dumas, the capital of his State. At the request of Maharaja Bhupender Singh, he went to Dumas, stayed there with the Nawab known as Esquire-Sultan and prepared an exhaustive plan for making Dumas into a big holiday resort. There he developed a very strong friendship with Nawab Hamidullah Khan and his Begum. He describes his stay at Dumas in his own words:

"Mahidullah Khan wanted to develop Dumas as a seaside

resort and asked Maharaja of Patiala to lend my services to him for a short while to plan the construction of Dumas as a holiday resort with a beautiful harbour and casino on the style of Monte Carlo and Las Vegas for the tourist, from India and all over the world, with a 5 star hotel, large roads and parks, and additional harbour for passenger ships.

"I stayed at Dumas for some months and as I had some experience of construction of sea side resorts and watering places and casinos, I planned it as a beautiful tourist centre. Its cost, according to my estimates, came to about twenty five crores of rupees. As the Nawab had no funds for such a venture, he asked some financiers from Bombay to help him achieve his ambition. In the meantime I was entertained by the Nawab in the most sumptuous way. Every evening he would get three chairs placed in a corner of his palace garden where the balmy breeze would blow straight front the sea. These three chairs were reserved for the Nawab and his favourite Begum Naseem and myself. The cool and lovely breeze from the tides and waves of the sea was most pleasant and refreshing. After enjoying the breeze for a short time and indulging in casual talk, the Nawab ordered for alcoholic drinks to be served to the Begum and myself and we were the only two of the three to be participating in these delicious and intoxicating drinks. The Nawab abstained from drinking the alcoholic beverages due to religious prejudices but he had no objection to his Begum sharing drinks with me. Usually the Begum and I had many drinks before dinner was served at about 10'o clock at night. She became my intimate friend. The Nawab seemed to accept my intimacy. The Nawab seemed to accept the fate sportingly. The chivalrous behaviour of his guests to his Begum did not cause a pang of jealousy in his heart. The scheme was excellent and would have paid dividends if businessmen had invested money in this project but knowing the dictatorial power which these rulers enjoyed at that time in the States, it was difficult for the financiers from India to invest money in a project like this. The Nawab later tried to raise money through the princely order but here also he did not succeed to allure his fellow Princes to this tempting proposition. It was sheer bad luck of the Nawab and the country that such an alluring project did not materialize. Dumas would have been, as planned by me, another Monte Carlo, Cannes or Las Vegas. Business apart, the Nawab was one of most courteous, sporting, chivalrous and romantic ruler whom I met in my long service in the Indian States. His hospitality was unique. He did not mind his Begum entertaining alone his personal and intimate guests with her charms and company at the dead of the night ending with a game of Ping Pong in the Chinese style."

Tourist Resorts

As a minister in Patiala, Jarmani Dass had developed many tourist places. Facilities for tourists had been provided at Fatehgarh Sahib, Patiala and Pinjore. The Government of India picked up these very places for developing "low income group" tourist stations. All the three centres in Patiala were known for their scenic setting, bewitching beauty and historical importance. Pinjore has a history dating back to Mahabharat and houses a garden which is an exact replica of the Shalimar garden of Srinagar. Patiala was an admixture of history and modernism. Its developed State museum and gardens attracted tourists in large numbers after independence. The old residents of the city remembered for a long time the good work done by Jarmani Dass.

As a Minister in charge of Health he was also responsible for Maharaja Bhupinder Singh's health. The Maharaja, however, was a very difficult patient. He suffered from hypertension. In spite of the advice of his physicians, he continued with his licentious life style. Many senior physicians and been called from France and the U.K. Prof. Abramian, close friend of Jarmani Dass, was paid rupees one lakh per month income tax free plus perks. He would go back when his job was over but was often prevailed upon to stay on. He had almost succeeded in curing the Maharaja and had gone back to Paris. Jarmani Dass was also away on tour. The Maharaja's condition worsened.

Maharaja Bhupinder Singh had a very high regard for Jarmani Dass. He loved, admired and trusted him. Once both played chess right throughout the night. The Maharaja lost very heavily. When he met him the next morning he called for the cheque book and asked Jarmani how much he owed him. Diwan Sahib refused to take the substantial amount that he had won in the game and told him that he would be satisfied with a cheque of one Anna. Which he could keep as a memento (Please see photograph).

After his marriage to Sushila, Diwan Jarmani Dass's last wife, the couple had arranged a banquet and invited Maharaja Bhupinder Singh of Patiala as the Chief Guest. Ducks and wines from Paris were also ordered. A few dancing belles of repute were also invited to entertain the Maharaja. The Maharaja in his grand speech hailed Jarmani and averred that inclusion of in his service was a gain of Patiala and a loss of Kapurthala.

In Kapurthala he had fallen a victim to a bigoted Muslim Prime Minister Sir Abdul Hamid's palace intrigues and conspiracies. Here in Patiala also he suffered at the hands of a bigoted Muslim Major Hamid Hasan Khan and Cap. Rashid who planned all sorts of conspiracies against him. The young

Yudvinder Singh was tricked into believing that Jarmani Dass had plotted with the Resident Sir Harold Wilberforce Bell for a consideration of Rs. 20,000 to dethrone the Maharaja. The Machiavellian mind of Major Hamid Hasan Khan, ADC to the Maharaja, supported by Bhai Burcharan Singh, a clerk working under him in the Privy Purse Department, had cooked up this.

Diwan Sahib's enemies were busy spreading rumours against him when Maharaja Bhupinder Singh was on the death bed. Befooling the young Maharaja was not a difficult task. As a young boy the heir apparent Yuvraj Yaduvinder Singh was kept under strict discipline by Diwan Jarmani Dass. He feared that his elder brother Maharama Kumar Brijendra Singh might dethrone him. When the conspiracy, referred to earlier in this chapter, was put into operation, it was found the gullible young Maharaja was quite eager to believe it. While the machination was hatched in Patiala, the forgery part of it was finalised in Bombay. An expert in forgery was engaged. The conspirators carried out their manoeuvres from Hotel Taj whose proprietor also sensed what the visitors from Patiala were upto.

Although everything was eventually cleared it was too late.

Diwan Sahib's typist suffered the worst torture but remained loyal to him. Both the typist Amar Nath Sharma and Superintendent Arjan Dass Bansal were detained in "Kare-Khas" (torture cell). Diwan Sahib was deeply distressed over this sordid episode. In order to give a befitting reply to the Maharaja, Jarmani Dass made it a point that he would resign from the State Service only after the release of these innocent employees. Jarmani Dass resigned from his job in sheer disgust and left Patiala on 7th November, 1939. After his resignation the faithful servants decorated his car with flowers. Palace watchers remarked that it was a sad occasion as Jarmani Dass bade farewell to an exalted and lucrative office. Jarmani Dass wanted to make a fresh start in life, away from the world of palace intrigues.

Stint as Assistant Censor, Government of India, 1941-1942

During his long tenure as Minister in Patiala and Kapurthala, he had developed close friendship with many senior officers of the British Indian Army. Besides many of his close friends from Sorbonne and Oxford had also risen very high in politics, army and administrative services. Lord Glancy, the Governor of Punjab was his friend. He had authorised him to give his name as a reference whenever he applied for a post anywhere in the British Empire. He had, therefore, no difficulty in joining the Censor Department of the Army. He declined a posting in Madras but accepted it in Bombay. The following letter from Ltd. Col. C.W. Holland speaks volumes about the high esteem enjoyed by him.

"This letter is to certify that Major Jarmani Dass, O.B.E. was employed in the Censorship Organisation as an Assistant Censor from 2-6-1941 to 24-3-1942.

He carried out his duties in an efficient and painstaking manner. He was offered a Commission but refused it for reasons. He left censorship as the Army Headquarters had decided that all gentlemen of his category should be commissioned or their services dispensed with.

It is understood that the private reasons referred to above were that he had hoped for a suitable civil appointment.

His stay at Bombay was a very short one but it proved very fruitful to him. Here he developed friendship with Seth Govind Ram Saksaria who was known as the Cotton King of India in the U.S.A. As Assistant Censor he had access to the information and used to advice Seth Govind Ram Saksaria who made full use of it commercially. Both became intimate friends. The Cotton King floated a company worth Rs. 25 lakhs as capital and made Jarmani Dass its Managing Director.

Women, Marriage And Sex

"I must confess that if I have lived to such a long life it is only due to you who has been sent to me by Providence. If you were not there I would have died 11 years ago at the age when my brother died or even earlier. You have taken good care of me and advised me to take proper diet and nursing."

Letter to LH from France.

Diwan Daulat Ram died at the age of 33 leaving behind four sons and a daughter. Diwan Sureshwer Dass, Diwan Wilayati Ram, Diwan Mankesher Dass and Diwan Jarmani Dass. Because of their noble lineage, the Maharaja of Kapurthala, Jagjit Singh, treated all the brothers like his own children. All the brothers were sent to Europe for higher education. Subsequently Diwan Sureshwer Dass became the Chief Justice of Kapurthala. He lived in a bungalow which had eighteen acres of land attached to it.

Diwan Wilayati Ram became the Superintending Engineer. His Patiala bungalow was known as the Red House. Diwan Jarmani Dass lived in an eight acres bungalow called Ambaltas. It was so called because a larger number of Ambaltas trees were growing in it. It is here that he used to receive national and international dignitaries like His Highness Sir Sultan Mohammed Shah, Agha Khan III, the Prince of Wales and other noted personalities of the time.

Kam Kandla or Kami as she was nick-named was engaged to Diwan Wilayati Ram, the elder brother of Diwan Jarmani Dass. As the latter had gone to U.K. for higher education in engineering and the parents of Kami were pressing for an early marriage, Jarmani Dass's mother persuaded him to marry her instead. Such was the respect shown to elders that the young Diwan agreed to the request of his widowed mother. The marriage, however, did not prove successful. For long spells of time, Diwan Jarmani Dass had to remain on tour abroad, with his Highness, the Maharaja of Kapurthala. Apart from age, there was the cultural and educational disparity. She was just simple homely girl not well educated to compete with Jarmani Dass. After sometime a daughter Brij Kishory was born who was later on married to Amrit Badhawar of Ujjain. Kami was given all the family jewellery, household articles, a handsome pension and a bungalow with an orchard at 32 Rajpur Road, Dehradun (U.P.). Thus she was properly separated and started living in style. With consent of Kami and Brij Kishori, Jarmani Dass agreed to marry another women Laila, daughter of the Turkish Grand Wazir.

Pasha's daughter becomes Leilawanti.

Among the numerous women who fell in love with him because of his ability, charming personality and affable nature Laila was considered to be the most beautiful woman of her times in the world. Her father, Wazir Izzet Pasha Al Abid, was a Minister in the Court of Sultan Afjaul Hamid of Turkey and also the right hand man of the Sultan. He was powerful enough to get his opponents in the court dismissed and thrown into the Bosphorous from the balcony overlooking the sea. After the revolution in Turkey, the Sultan and his chief adviser Izzet Pasha were exiled to Salonica. Being a close confidante of the Sultan Wazir had amassed fabulous wealth. Even in exile he lived like a king. He brought up his daughter Laila in great luxury and comforts and gave her the best education through European, Turkish and Arabic tutors. She could speak English, French, Spanish apart from Arabic fuently. Often she dressed in European clothes and, occasionally in Turkish dress with a veil in transparent silk - through which one could see her face. With her exquisite beauty, figure and culture she was a superb specimen of feminine grace. She lived in the most fashionable part of Paris with her mother. It was at a hotel called Chateau de Madrid that she first met Jarmani Dass. It was a case of love at first sight which soon turned into infatuation and complete surrender. Laila persuaded him to marry her at a seaside resort where both had gone for a holiday.

The marriage was performed according to Vedic rites by an Arya Samajist Priest Swami Diwan Chand Verma "Yogi" who had settled in France to practise "Pranotherapy". This Swami became famous in France where he lived till 1931. In 1937, he packed up for London where he settled at 11 Wellington Court, Knights Bridge, S.W.I. The same year his first book in English was published. Later on the marriage contract was drawn up and signed by both the parties in the presence of many eminent witnesses. According to this contract Laila renounced her Muslim faith and pledged to carry out her new Vedic faith in all respects. It is signed by her as Lemma Laila Izzet. This marriage took place on August 3, 1924. She never forgot this date in her life. She considered it the most auspicious day in her life. Her infatuation for Diwan Sahib was complete. She had been given the name Leilawanti of which she was very proud. Maharaja Jagjit Singh of Kapurthala did not relish the idea of Diwan Sahib's getting married to Laila as he thought this would hinder him in his duties towards him. According to the numerous letters and telegrams available on record, Laila travelled to various countries in disguise with Diwan Sahib without the knowledge of the Maharaja. Her stay at luxury hotels and in ships was pre-arranged with meticulous care. She had the mind and heart of a poet. After leaving one part, she pined for the next. Her travels and travails and sorrows and the ultimate dissolution of marriage are narrated by Diwan Sahib in his own inimitable style.

"On our return to Europe, on a French Steamer called "lie De France", she also had a double berthed deluxe cabin in the same steamer and came on board incognito and unseen by the Maharaja, as she used to shut herself the whole day and night in her luxurious cabin. I had a cabin in my name, but I spent most of my time with Laila in her cabin. When we reached Paris, the Maharaja was pleased with me because of my obedience to his wishes and for leaving behind Laila in Paris."

"Laila's adventures with me became known to Izzet Pasha who was living at that time in Cairo in exile. He divorced his wife and disinherited Laila. Their allowances were stopped and they did not have any means of livelihood. I had to supply funds to them in accordance with my means. Whenever I came to Paris or passed through Cairo I paid her debts and left her sufficient funds for several months' expenditure. Whatever savings I used to make were spent on clearing the debts of Laila which ran into thousands of pounds. This state of affairs went on for many years and my fortune was nearly exhausted."

Wazir Izzet Pasha who was already 76 years of age got seriously ill with a serious attack of gout and other complications and was on death bed. Laila left Paris for Cairo with her mother to be near her father. With her usual charm and tact, she penetrated into the bedroom of her father and began to nurse him. After her visit to Mecca, Izzet Pasha's heart was already softened towards Laila and her mother, and on the request of Laila, the Sultan of Hedjas intervened on behalf of Laila to bring about a reconciliation between the father and her mother. A few days before his death, Izzet Pasha forgave her and her mother and she became one of the legal heirs to her father's big fortune amounting to several millions of pounds sterling. A few months after the death of Wazir Izzet Pasha, she decided to visit India.

"I met her in Bombay where I reserved for her a suite of rooms in the Taj Mahal Hotel. In Bombay an old personal friend Mr. M.A. Jinnah, who afterwards became the Governor General of Pakistan when India was partitioned, entertained us to dinner and was pleased at this alliance. Mrs. Sarojini Naidu, who is who is considered to be one of the greatest women in this epoch and has played a pivotal role in India's Independence movement, blessed our union and invited us to tea at her suite of rooms at the Taj Mahal Hotel."

"From Bombay we went to Mysore after visiting Poona for a couple of days. His Highness the Yuvraj of Mysore, who was personal friend of mine, received us at Bangalore and put us up at the magnificent place, Jay Mahal, as his guests."

"Sir Mirza Ismail, Prime Minister of Mysore, gave a banquet in our honour to which he invited most of the important members of the society in Bangalore as well as ministers and high officials. From Bangalore we went to Mysore by car accompanied by the then His Highness the Yuvraj of Mysore. The journey was comfortable and did not take more than a few hours to reach Mysore. Again we were put up at the best guest house usually reserved for the Viceroys and the distinguished guests of Maharaja. The Maharaja received us at his Palace and entertained us to a dinner party though he did not eat anything himself, being a strictly orthodox Hindu who would take his food alone in a special room devoid of all furniture and sprinkled with Ganges water to make it sacred and pure."

"The dinner party was followed by music, conducted by the famous musicians of Mysore. About 70 to 80 men with Indian musical instruments such as Veena, Sitar, Jaltarang and similar oriental musical instruments were playing the tunes. The Palace was illuminated and the whole town celebrated our visit to the State. We were taken to Chaumundi Goddess Temple which is on the top of a hill, six or seven miles from Mysore. This temple was electrified and the whole route was lit on both sides with electric lamps. It was a sight worth seeing when from that temple one looked at the Palace and the town."

"A thrilling fight between two elephants was shown to us during our visit there. The elephants were ferocious and both were intoxicated for fighting ferociously. After a few hours of fighting the elephant of the Maharaja beat the elephant of the Yuvraj, whose elephant fled away before an audience of seven thousand people crying and howling loudly. It was caught with great difficulty after being spread many times by the cavalry men who stood in the arena and followed the defeated elephant so that it may not attack the passersby."

"Laila and I also visited Banaras, the sacred city of the Hindus. There she was accosted by the astrologers and palmists who predicted that she would not make India her home. The burning ghats made her very gloomy and depressed though the Maharaja of Banaras entertained us lavishly and a large special barge with silk lining and liveried boatmen was placed at our disposal and we were put up in Nandesar Palace. This Palace is generally reserved for distinguished guests, such as Viceroys, heads of foreign governments and the Maharajas."

"A magnificent garden in 15 to 20 acres of land with water flowing all around like the Mughal Gardens surrounded the palace. It was built of marble and it was there that King Edward VII and other British Monarchs stayed whenever they visited the State. The Palace was specially constructed for the visit of King Edward to Banaras at the time of his coronation."

"From Banaras we went to Kapurthala where the Maharaja had ordered that street lights should remain on even after midnight as the train which brought us to Kapurthala arrived at about five in the morning. Normally the lights were put off after midnight for economic reasons. The lights were on when we entered the city and special waiters in gorgeous uniforms were sent from the Palace to serve breakfast and special food at my house called "Ambaltas" which was furnished in modern European style. The garden looked picturesque with multi-coloured flowers and tropical plants. My eldest brother Diwan Sureshwer Dass, Chief Justice of the State, gave a grand reception to Laila the same afternoon while my mother and the high priest of my family performed religious ceremonies which were customary when the bride entered her husband's home for the first time. After all the religious ceremonies were over, Laila was entertained to a largely attended garden party given by the citizens to welcome her to the town. She wore jewellery worth two million rupees. Diamond rings adorned her slim, beautiful fingers. She bought this jewellery after the death of her father and also inherited other rare stones from her father's property.

"Maharaja Jagjit Singh of Kapurthala had ordered a special golden dinner service set which he presented to her when she visited the palace. She received many valuable presents from my various Rajas and friends and relatives throughout India, and the Yuvraj of Mysore, the Maharaja of Rajpipla, the Maharaja Sayaji Rao Gaekwad of Baroda, Mr. M. A. Jinnah, Maharaja of Banaras, His Highness Agha Khan and others. Mr. R. D. Tata, father of Mr. J. R. D. Tata, Chairman Tata concerns, who was a personal friend of mine also entertained us to a dinner in Bombay on our arrival to which he had also invited Mr. M. A. Jinnah and Mr. R. D. Sethna and many other important political leaders and business magnates. Mr. R. D. Tata presented Laila with a valuable ring set with a big ruby. Seeing the presents offered to Laila, the Maharajas of other States were very keen to give her more presents."

"The Maharaja arranged a special reception at the Jagjit Palace, Kapurthala, a replica of Versailles in Paris, in her honour on the day following our arrival at Kapurthala."

"The Prime Minister Sir Abdul Hamid, who was a bigoted Muslim, was perplexed to see that the Maharaja was taking so much interest in the reception of the wife of a Minister who was not on friendly terms with him. He was also furious on account of a Muslim woman embracing Hinduism by marrying a Hindu, though Sir Abdul Mahid's great grandfather was a convert from Hinduism to Islam, as it was the usual practice during the Mughal period with millions of people."

"Over one-fifth of the population of India was formerly converted perforce from Hinduism to Islam by Aurangzeb, the last Mughal Emperor. The Muslims who were converted from Hinduism became more bigoted and fanatical than the original inhabitants of Turkey, Arabia, Egypt and Afghanistan and other Muslim countries."

"Sir Abdul Hamid's great grandfather – a Sehgal was a high caste Hindu. The members of this family, particularly in the Punjab, held high places, not only in the administrative service of the Government of India and the Government of Indian States, but in professions like commerce, industry, legal profession and others."

"Sir Abdul Hamid did not possess any of the family traits after 2 or 3 generations of conversion and he was boiling with rage to see the daughter of Izzet Pasha having been converted to Hinduism. Unfortunately, for her and myself, Swami Shradha Nand, a great spiritual leader and reformer, was assassinated by a Muslim fanatic just before the arrival of Laila in India. The Swami's cult was to preach that there should be redical reforms in Hindu society and culture, and advocated the conversion of Muslim to the Hindu faith in the same way as the Muslims had resorted before to the wholesale conversions of Hindus."

"The Swami's fanatical reforms gave impetus to the agitation against Laila, conducted by the Muslims at the Railway Stations and the cities which she visited. When Sir Abdul Hamid was introduced by the Maharaja to Laila, he showed the venom of his hatred in the presence of the Maharaja and hundreds of other people and told her that she had no place in India, nor would she be received in this country by the Muslims or Hindus. The bigoted Muslims did not like the idea of a Hindu marrying a Mohammedan women of such high family and pure Muslim blood not knowing that the Hindu religious rights were observed by us due to sheer necessity of peculiar circumstances in which we were placed and not due to fanaticism or proselytisation on my part."

"In Delhi, His Holiness Pir Hassan Nizami Sujjadanshin Dargah Hazarat Nizam-ud-in Aulia, a well-known Muslim religious leader, expressed his disapproval of this alliance, though he was a personal friend of mine and knew my liberal ideas. Some Muslims also sent astrologers to her at the Maidens Hotel, Delhi, where we were staying during our stay in the capital, to tell her that this alliance was fraught with danger to her life and future. Many times I saw her weeping and lamenting over her fate."

"Laila was much distressed by this trend of public

opinion and gave up the idea of staying in India. Some of the newspapers began to indulge in malicious propaganda by disapproving of her marriage to a Hindu, and many Muslim organisations vehemently opposed it. When I complained to the Maharaja against the behaviour of Abdul Hamid, he took no action. On the contrary, he was pleased that this communal antagonism of the people might cause a rift in our relationship and induce Laila to leave the country for good."

"Laila and I left Kapurthala for a short trip and after visiting Delhi for a few days went to Bombay. Here she proposed that I should give up the Maharaja's service and stay with her by going round on a world tour at her expense. She had by now inherited a big fortune of several crores of rupees on the death of her father Wazir Izzet Pasha, who having escaped from being caught by the Young Turks had begun to live in Cairo in a luxurious house."

"My marriage with Laila was kept a secret from Wazir Izzet Pasha for a long time though he come to know it two years before his death. After knowing this, he disinherited her though he was reconciled with her just a few days before his death. Having inherited a big fortune with plenty of money, she bought big residential houses in Paris, London, and other places and it was only after the death of Wazir Izzet Pasha that she could visit India as my legally married wife."

"When Laila was leaving for Europe, the Maharaja gave me leave only for a few days to see her off at Bombay. On the way we stopped at Delhi and she threatened to commit suicide by throwing herself from the third floor of Maidens Hotels where we had taken an apartment, if I did not accompany her to Europe."

"I told her that it was not possible for me to do so without the permission of the Maharaja. Thereupon, she brought out a cheque of Rs. 50 lakhs and threw it at my feet and said that this cheque of Rs. 50 lakhs should cover more than I would get for years and years by serving the Maharaja."

"Infatuated though I was with her glamorous beauty as well as her depth of affection and love for me, I tore up the cheque and told her that no amount of money could wean me away from doing my duty towards the Maharaja. However, I told her that I would try to accompany her to Paris and would ask the Maharaja for further leave. I sent a telegram to the Maharaja for extension of leave and the Maharaja, as was expected, turned it down. This telegram was received by me at Mathura Railway Station and when I opened the telegram Laila read the contents and she jumped from the running train which had started to move and fell on the platform. I stopped the train by pulling the alarm cord. As the train was not running fast, she only got serious bruises on her face and body. Seeing her condition and firm resolve to take me to Europe, I sent another telegram to the Maharaja and expected a reply at Bombay. The Maharaja again disagreed with my request but due to pressure on him by some personal friends of mine, to whom he listened, the Maharaja half-heartedly agreed to extend my leave for a month and a half and ordered that I should meet him in Marseilles on his next visit to Europe.

"There were objections from the religious leaders of the Muslim community that such a marriage was not possible and not permissible to a Hindu married man. It became a socio-religions problem and topic of that day. Thus Laila left India. Laila's mind was made up to quit this country for ever and on the way to Europe she was unhappy and always talked of the ill treatment she had received in India, both from my people and from the Muslim community. After the expiry of my leave, I had to go and meet the Maharaja at Marseilles when he disembarked there. "

"The first question he asked me was whether I was still with Laila. I replied, "Yes, your Highness, Laila is with me." The Maharaja felt annoyed. The Maharaja was planning to travel to various parts of Europe and he made up his mind to take me along and to separate me from Laila. This infuriated her more and ultimately, she began to believe that the astrologers's predictions were coming true. The astrologers in India were bribed by some Muslims to say such irritating things to her so that she should get disgusted with myself and India."

"I was fighting between love and duty as well as the fate of hundreds of my relatives and friends who could be in serious trouble if incurred the Maharaja's displeasure. So, I inclined my life at her expenses. By nature I was so made that I could not possibly live on a woman's gifts. Throughout the period of my stay with Laila in Europe, America and India I did not let her spend a farthing from her own pocket when she was travelling with me. In this way I was a real oriental and a man."

Leilawanti received many threats from the fanatical Muslims of India. It was made clear to her that she would be murdered for renouncing her faith and marrying a Hindu. Her life became miserable and she decided to leave for Europe. Diwan Jarmani Dass hid her passport which she managed to recover with the fraudulent help of Diwan Mankeshwar Dass who charged rupees ten thousand from Laila.

There are many episodes of this story, but a few of them are really shocking. Laila after her departure from India, which was made possible by Diwan Mankeshwar Dass by stealing Laila's passport and handing over to her.

The second episode relates to the "Great Search". After getting rid of Laila, Diwan Jarmani Dass went to Palampur now in Himachal Pradesh took refuge in isolation before he joined the service of the His excellency the Maharaja of Patiala.

He had passed through the period of suspense and sent out his loyal agents almost from every community to every direction to search a suitable match for him. This was a period of trial and error but he succeeded finally. After staying with him Carl Holmes went to Lahore and stayed at Falettis. Those who volunteered to depose for him were paid Rs. 500 each. Besides Diwan Pearey Lal and S.C. Judge Mr.

Chambers and counsellor at Law, Mr. William. Wadhams also came to India. Scotland yard was also associated with the investigation. In spite of all these efforts and huge expenditure by Mr. Holmes, Laila won the case because bigamy could not be proved. Diwan Jarmani Dass did not go to court but it was proved that he had never married Laila.

Eligible Bachelor Again

His first wife Bibi Kam Kandla was most simple and the second one more educated. Now he wanted to tread the middle path and settle down with a homely but smart wife. He had two bitter experience. Sometime passed between his second wife and the third one. It is said that a boatman's Hokah (traditional smoking instrument) never remains Sookhan (dry). During this period he came into contact with an English girl who he called Shakuntala. It shown that Shakuntala had a long affair with him but nobody knows where or who she was. He thought of marrying her but she left for Europe leaving many moments for him. In this all his friends and Maharanis joined hands. There was one Swarn Lata daughter of Lala Goverdhan Dass of Sunlife Insurance Co. When he went to see her she started playing the record on the Gramophone whose strain was "I love you". Diwan Sahib left the house there and than in spite of her parents lavish display of jewellery and sumptuous food. She felt so desperate the she resolved to be a nun and never marry. Sometimes after, the proposal fell through and she became a sum and never married anyone in life.

There was one Mr. Har Sukh Rai, who along with his daughter used to permanently stay at Flattis (Lahore) the poshest hotel in Punjab. At that time he was keen that Jarmani Dass marry his daughter. Ram Rattan of Gilgit suggested many matches. Similarly Master Dev Raj, the tutor, came forward with many proposals. One of his relations Shri Amrit Lal Sehgal, Member, Income Tax Tribunal, was interested in Diwan Sahib for his sister Kamla (Later Mrs. Kamla Dhingra).

Diwan Mankeshwar Dass offered him his wife's sister who was the daughter of Mehta Arjun Das of Amritsar. Even his first wife Bibi Kam Kandla offered her brother's daughter. Shri B.P.L. Bedi also came forward with a proposal but nothing came out of it.

The Lahore Connection:

There was a Sadhu Maharaja at Lahore who was frequently visited by the Sushila's maternal grandmother Bibi Lurindi Kapur. One day Shri Surinder Singh Bedi, an agent of Diwan Jarmani Dass, asked the great Mahatma to suggest a suitable match for Diwan Sahib. Bibi Lurindi overheard and suggested the name of her second granddaughter Sushila. The outcome was that Mahatma, Bedi, Lurindi and her woman friend set out in a car for Wazirabad where Sushila's father, Lala Shiv Das, a freedom fighter and an Assistant Editor of *Tribune* and Principal of a school at Lahore. It took them quite a lot of time to persuade Sushila's father for an audience with Diwan Jarmani Dass. Her father was reluctant for obviously two reasons. Firstly Diwan Sahib was a divorcee. Secondly he did not like his daughter to be disapproved by Diwan Sahib. Ultimately the father yielded. Thereby the party insisted for the matrimonial alliance of Sushila with Diwan Jarmani Dass.

Sushila belonged to a well-known nationalist family of Lahore. Her father was a freedom fighter and social reformer. He worked as Assistant Editor of Tribune. He was also Principal of a school in Lahore. One of his books *The Industrial Encyclopaedia* was published by renowned Messrs. D.B. Taraporewala & Co. of Bombay who used to remit the royalty to him regularly. Sushila Devi had studied at the Arya Kanya Putri Pathashala and at Queen Victoria Girls High School, Lahore, an English medium public school, where speaking in Hindi was strictly banned. She passed her Matriculation from this School. The former school imparted a strong nationalist and moral trait to her character and the latter made her exceptionally smart and her command over English became very strong. Later on she passed her B.A. as a private candidate.

The interview was held at a friend's house at Gujranwala. At night a snake slithered past her without harming her in any way. It was interpreted as a very good omen. Sushila's maternal uncle had also appeared on the scene but was upset at the going on. Diwan Sahib arrived at the House at Gujranwala in the evening and was ushered in to a room, where Sushila's parents were waiting to receive him. After a free and frank talk, it was decided to introduce Sushila to Diwan Sahib who appeared on the scene, where her grandmother alongwith her friend and Diwan Sahib were present. After clarification of some vital issues they consented to marry each other. Both got married in November 7, 1936 at Gujranwala. The barat (marriage party) came from Kapurthala. For Sushila it was love at first sight and for Diwan Sahib it was yet another conquest. After the marriage the couple stayed at Flattis at Lahore and then left for Patiala where Diwan Kahn Chand, the Revenue Minister (1888-1946) played the role of a father in-law. A grand feast was arranged at Patiala for which special delicacies were imported from Paris. It was attended by all the luminaries of the state including the Maharaja Bhupinder Singh. Later the couple went to Kapurthala where further religious rites were performed and prayers were performed in the Gunidwara situated in the family house.

This marriage proved eminently successful. Sushila stood by him through thick and thin. She took due care of his health, financial matters and social obligations. He followed his literary pursuits and she spent her time in social work. One was the L.H. (Loving Husband) and the other the L.H. (Light of Heart). In some respect both were poles apart. If one was the north the other was the south pole. But they did not allow their difference to spoil their harmonious family life. On October 5, 1970 he wrote the following note for L.R. which according to him was the dictation of God, Almighty.

"I will never abuse you,

I will never distrust you,

I will behave like I behaved during first 20 years of life.

I should be forgiven if I annoyed you in any way.

It is not my fault. I do not mean to hurt you.

I wish you happiness and bliss all my love till the end of my life"

To Sushila, Your L.H.

The marriage proved to the world that even when the partners are poles part, they can lead a harmonious, happy married life provided they have the capacity to adjust.

These remarks were necessitated by the successive ailments which made him repent for his follies.

Delink Religion from Politics

These days there is lot of talk about separating religion from politics. Their nexus at present is leading the country to ruin. As early as on October 15, 1931, Diwan Jarmani Dass addressed a circular to the political leaders and intellectuals of the country exhorting them not to mix politics with religion. It was addressed to the leaders of various political parties who had gathered at London to attend the Second Round Table Conference. The letter signed by him under the pseudonym "Yogi" is reproduced below:

"Your object in coming over here was to obtain absolute freedom for India, without which, you felt that it was impossible for you to possess political, religious, or economic liberty. Once the Government of India is in your hands, you feel that you will be able to reorganise the education, commerce, health and politics of the country."

"Since an alien government has not given you justice you have decided to free your country at all costs from foreign oppression."

"It is a great problem and one which can only be resolved if you maintain a united front."

"Let all parties join as one, whatever their beliefs, and without distinction of religion, cases or colour."

"Most religions seek their own freedom without caring much about that of other's religions. You are even ready to call in foreign aid to protect your own particular interests. This method of dividing India into different warring factions was the cause of its downfall. Now that you feel that you are about to regain your freedom you will admit that India needs to make much progress if it is to be on the same level as other nations."

"It is most unfortunate for the country that you are asking for separate electorate according to your separate religious beliefs. A certain part is asking that the majority be confined to the provinces. This is contrary to the political custom of every other country, for no country ever votes according to its different religious beliefs. If the Protestants, Catholics, Jews and orthodox communities in England each wished to have a separate electorate it would mean the ruin of the English political system. Religion and politics have nothing in common. Religion develops concern, the collectivity, their business is to protect the country against rebellion or invasion."

"At the present moment the world is in a state of economic discord. In Europe, there is a movement towards unity and confederation, disarmament and universal peace.

But in India your political methods tend to foster hatred among your countrymen and bring about religious wars."

"The eyes of the whole world are now fixed upon you the leaders of the oldest and most civilised nation on earth. A country which has been the homeland of all, that is spiritual, has the perfect right to its liberty. By stirring up religious strife you show that you are incapable of governing yourselves and need an alien government to impose order."

"This is a ridiculous state of affairs for a country which ought to become the model of spiritual democracy for the whole world."

"India is destined to establish such a spiritual democracy based upon the qualities of head and heart, and taking a lead in this venture would mean serving the whole world at a moment when such qualities are most needed of all."

The Quit India Movement

9th August, 1942 is an important date and marks a watershed in the turbulent history of India. On this day Mahatma Gandhi launched his Quit India Movement. Mahatma Gandhi had planned it as a moral movement to pressurise the British and finally to force them to leave the country. Many Congressmen did as they were expected to do. Many protests were peaceful. In Bihar the movement took an ugly turn. Repression was let loose on peaceful processionists. There were agent - provocateurs who saw to it that there were violent incidents. As a result of bureaucratic tyranny, the law and order machinery in Bihar completely collapsed. The nationalist minded masses formed a sort of parallel government over there. There were widespread disturbances in other parts of the country as well. Outside the country, however, little was known about the political unrest. Censor was imposed and strictly enforced. No news was allowed to go out. Under such circumstances Mrs. Vijayalakshmi Pandit managed to leave the country for the USA. It was in 1943 that she launched a massive propaganda campaign against the British imperialist designs in India. To counter her campaign the British approached Jarmani Dass. They offered him a fat salary if he could go to the USA and stern the tide of anti-imperialist propaganda. He rejected the offer with all the contempt that it deserved. He was not prepared to utter against his country. After his point blank refusal the British made the offer to Sardar K.M. Pannikar who readily accepted it. It is not known how he performed the dirty job but he did go to the USA. Sardar Pannikar was a man of great ability. Probably it became clear to him that the British were on the verge of quitting the country. The Sardar came back to India and got the job of Prime Minister in Bikaner State. It was a very wise political somersault on his part. Bikaner, because of KM. Pannikar, was the first State to integrate with free India. He later on became a member of the States Reorganisation Committee (SRC) and helped Sardar Patel in the colossal task of reorganisation of States.

As a Prolific Writer of English Prose

He was a keen observer of life. He had a deep knowledge of history of the places he visited. His imagination was that of a poet but he had the observant eye of a scientist. When he penned down his experiences, he did not lose sight of details. His descriptions are not based on hearsay but on very keen personal observations. Exaggeration was unknown and incongruent to his nature. Everything that he stated in his books had documentary evidence fortified by eye-witness accounts. When he wrote the book "Maharaja" he had been warned by his friend Sardar K.M. Pannikar that he would soon be garlanded with a series of defamation cases. But this was not to be. Even Stella whose story is one of the most interesting and damaging one in "Maharaja" came down to Delhi from U.K. to threaten him with a defamation case but had to beat a hasty retreat when it dawned on her that even the smallest detail in her story of sexual exploitation of the prince was based on facts known and noted by him. When it came to describing an event, his language match the occasion. The effect was dramatic, the choice of word was appropriate and the style so real and natural that it looked like author was narrating a personal experience sitting by the fireside with mastery and effortless ease. He never used any vulgar word even when he was attacking vulgarity. He had travelled around the world several times during the days when travel was not fast. He had to remain outside the country for months together. He had visited most of the countries of South America, along with Europe, Africa and Asia. Jagjit Singh went to Indonesia, China, Japan, Indo-China, Siam, Malaya and many other Eastern countries. He has left a vivid account of some of places he visited. In his book "The Wonders of Panam" he described in minute detail how the engineering marvel of world works. A pertinent paragraph from the book is quoted below:

"The whole scheme was overhauled and re-examined and the original route considerably altered before the actual work of construction was taken in hand, which cost commercial 375 million dollars and was finally opened to commercial traffic in 1914. The Gatun lake, which is formed by damming the Charges river is 85 ft. above sea level is made by means of the Pedro mignel locks. The whole process of ascent and descent is of such absorbing interest that watched it more carefully from the Captain's bridge throughout our passage through the Canal. The three lock-chambers are each 1,000 ft. in length, 110 ft. in width and 70 ft. deep so as to accommodate quite easily the biggest liner or an-of-war in the world. The colossal lock gates are electrically operated, and the fender chains for opening and closing the valves are all controlled by an elaborate system of machinery worked with electric power. With incredible rapidity in the shortest possible time the lock-chamber is filled or emptied as required and the steamer passes into the adjoining part of the Canal. The whole process is gone through in is the utmost silence and everything accomplished with the greatest accuracy and speed. The so-called 'Canal Zone' which runs five miles each side of the Canal, is under American occupation where a fairly large garrison of 15,000 men is maintained for the protection of the Canal, whereas the rest is under the Republic of Panama."

He followed the ideal of correctness throughout his writings. A streak of humour runs through his works even while he is talking of serious matters. Accuracy of description couched in precise terminology is usually the quality of a scientist, that quality was almost a master passion with him. He faithfully describes even the smallest detail with remarkable accuracy.

The dates of historical events told by him are remarkably correct. The following passage from Maharani can be cited as an example of his faithful and accurate reporting:

"Before I proceed further, it may be of interest to know about the gallery of glasses where this Treaty was signed. The gallery of glasses was used daily by the king as a passage on special occasions to receive ambassadors of foreign countries. It is 73 metres in length, 10.50 metres in width and 12.30

metres in height, and became of historical significance because of many events such as of the presentation of the Ambassador of Siam in 1686 and Ambassador of Persia (Iran) in 1875, the marriage of Duke of Bourgoyne with Marie Adelaide de Savoie in 1897, the fancy masked ball on the occasion of the marriage of Marie Antoinette with Dauphin in 1770, proclamation of the Emperor of Germany in 1871 and finally, the signature of the Treaty of Versailles."

"It is an amusing historical fact that when the Ambassador of Siam presented his credentials to the King in the gallery of glasses in 1636, he had to crawl on his stomach for 73 metres and after the presentation of the credentials had to crawl back in the same way, keeping his face towards the king and not his back as a mark of respect for the King. The Ambassador must have been an athlete and strong man. It was a manifestation of the staunch loyalty of the King of Siam to the King of France".

Accolades from Abroad

It is said about Jarmani Dass that whoever came in contact with him became his admirer. He had travelled around the world extensively and come in contact with many Heads of State and other luminaries of the time. The result was that he was highly honoured by the States of Patiala, Kapurthala and Bahawalpur. The British conferred upon him the title of order of the British Empire (officer) for services rendered at the League of Nations. Other countries which decorated him were Spain, Egypt, Persia (Iran), Abbyssinia, Morocco, France, Chile, Cuba, Rumania St. Marmo and the Vatican. The titles received by him from the various countries are depicted on the jacket.

Integration of Princely Order

Since Jarmani Dass intimately connected with the administration of the States and their rulers, it would be appropriate to mention here what they were like. The 562 States were referred to as Indian, India, as distinct from the British India. In the maps of India of those days they were shown in yellow patches and the British India in red. Two-fifths of India's population lived in these States which covered an area of 600,000 square miles. The British had divided them into three main classes. First there were salute States. Their number being 118. Their rulers were entitled to firing guns on formal occasions. The King Emperor was entitled to 101 gun salutes, Viceroy 31. In that order of precedence the number of guns fired came down to 9. So great was the craze for titles and salutes that the rulers vied with each other for going up in the order of precedence. They spent lavishly in trying to receive more and better titles from the Viceroy and the King Emperor. The British officers of the political department used to get huge bribes from the princes for increasing the number of the guns salutes. When Diwan Sahib made arrangements for a banquet in honour of Lord Willingdon, Viceroy of India. (1931-1936), gave precedence to the Maharaja of Patiala over the Maharaja of Bikaner. This created an uproar and Diwan sahib was called by the Viceroy in the company of the Maharaja and asked to change the table plan. Although they were referred to as Indian India, there was hardly any feeling for India so far as the rulers were concerned. They were autocrats who spent the hard-earned revenues of the States they ruled on wine and women of Europe while their poor subjects languished in abject poverty. Mahatma Gandhi had called this system which allowed these despots to continue in power as the "Greatest blot on British rule in India." The States served as a bastion of British imperialism in India. The freedom fighters were treated in miserable manner. In most cases the ancestors of the rulers were the people who had betrayed the country and sided with the invaders. No wonder the rulers during the British times spent their time in buttering British master, or even their agents.

Integration of States

During 1947, Diwan Jarmani Dass was in great demand with nationalist leaders and senior officials of the States Department which had been entrusted with the colossal task of integrating the States. Since he was thoroughly conversant with the background of States and knew several of the princes and the Prime Ministers, his advice was very much sought after and appreciated. Earlier he had predicated that the spineless rulers of Indian States would integrate once the protective hand of the British was finally withdrawn. They had come into existence by supporting the invaders of the foreign powers at one critical time or the other. Most of them had supported the idea of perpetuating the privy purses. At this critical time was published the "*Maharaja*" which greatly strengthened the hands of Indira Gandhi who succeeded in finishing the privy purses and privileges once and for all.

Princely Resurgence

Certain forces were again trying to glorify the princes and belittle the achievements of the representatives of the common people of India. The ex-princes were even being painted as great patriots which is far from truth. The new generation is not well-versed with this period of our history. Attractive and colourful publication with during titles are being brought out by publishers which aim at promoting a certain nostalgia for the bygone era of the "Raj" and the Rajas. These evil designs need to be frustrated. Diwan Jarmani Dass has left several notes on the political conditions in the States long before their merger. It would be appropriate to give illuminating excerpts from some of his notes.

"The birth of the Indian National Congress was a challenge, big enough to set all the shrewd minds thinking. So Lord Lytton (Viceroy, 1876-80) had long ago advocated the formation of a Council of Princes to combat that challenge. Though that project of his was destined to materialise later, it was nevertheless, made a policy to boost them up on every occasion the national movement demanded anything. The doors of the States were closed to all progress, civilization and enlightenment, and it was the mighty watchmen of the British imperialism who scrupulously guarded them against the nationalist forces."

"Lytton's dream of making the States as the dens of reaction was being realised by various measures. Special laws were passed in British India to ensure against the "rebellious" or libellous propaganda against the Indian Princes. The policy of fraternization was beginning to crystallise by inviting the Princes for consultations and by giving them honours on special occasions."

"The worth of the Princes was not realised and was given expression to in various statements coming from the paramount power! Lord Harding called them Helpers and colleagues in the great task of imperial rule and hence the need arose for a regular body of the rulers to make the help and assistance easier. Even as early as 1906, Lord Minto had written to his successor Lord Morley, in his letter of May 26, 1906. 'I have been thinking a good deal lately of a possible counterpoise to Congress aims. I think we may find a solution in Council of Princes.'"

The worth of the worthless, became the pet theme of every wise imperialist, who wanted to impress upon the British public, to look upon their Indian slave master princes as really 'useful instruments of the Royal policy', thus spoke Prof L. F. Rushbrook Williams, Ex-Director of Public Information, Government of India, and retired Foreign Minister of Patiala:

"The situation of these feudal States, checker-boarding all India as they do, are a great safeguard. It is like stabilising a vast network of friendly fortresses in a debatable territory. It would be difficult for a general rebellion against the British to sweep through India because of this network of friendly powers."

Pandit Nehru on Indian States

We should know something of the conditions of the people in the States. Here nobody could say better than Pt. Nehru, who in his autobiography remarks:

"A sense of oppression comes, it is stifling and difficult to breathe, and below the still or low moving waters there is stagnation vividly with the glaring ostentation of the Prince's palace. How much of the wealth of the State flows into the palaces for the personal needs and luxuries of the princes, how little goes back to the people in the form of any service."

"A veil of mystery surrounds these States. Newspapers are not encouraged there, and at the most a literary or semi-official weekly flourish. Foreign newspapers are often banned. Literacy is very low, except in some of the Southern States, Travancore, Cochin, etc."

The Principal news that comes from a State is of a Viceregal visit with all its pomp and ceremonial and mutually complimentary speeches. Or, of an extravagantly celebrated marriage or birthday of the ruler or an agrarian rising. Special laws protect the princes from criticism, even in British India, and "within the States the mildest criticism is vigorously suppressed. Public meetings purposes are often banned."

Another writer has aired with an equal, if not more vehement wrath:

"It is impossible to imagine a more sensitive body than our Indian feudatories. They are consumed by petty jealousies among themselves, and of the strength of their armies. The example of one chief is infectious, the other cannot be outdone, and democracy is compromised so long as it has mere 500 autocrats as its allies. The Princes can render Great Britain a real service when they can offer their resources not as so many autocrats but as true representatives of their people."

Scuttling of a Conspiracy

As early as 1930-31, the British tried to organise the princes into a strong confederation. If the idea had been put into practice the merger of States that took place 16 years later would have become difficult even for a man like Sardar Patel (The Bismark and Garibaldi of India). This idea was mooted by some princes and British officials during the second session of Round Table Conference but was scuttled by Diwan Jarmani Dass with the help of Shri M.R. Jayakar, an eminent lawyer of Bombay. This little known fact of history is the greatest contribution of Diwan Jarmani Dass to the freedom movement which deserves to be written in bold letters. The result of the scuttling was that the princes had to remain content with the Chamber of Princes. This was dissolved in 1947. Diwan Sahib has very interesting observations to make about the dissolution of this chamber. They are as follows:

Dissolution of the Chamber of Princes

"There was a split between the ruling Princes with regard to the future set-up of the Government of India. It came to a head when the Nawab of Bhopal, Chancellor of the Chamber of Princes, resigned and H.H. the Maharaja of Patiala was asked the Viceroy to officiate as Chancellor. The Nawab of Bhopal and other Princes started a Movement for the formation of the Union of Princes and deserted the Chamber of Princes. This move initiated by the other Princes who had joined before did not evince any interest or show further co-operation. A winding up committee was formed to liquidate the organisation of the chamber of princes, with the Maharajas of Patiala, Bikaner, Jam Sahib of Pannikar as it member. The Committee was instructed to wind up the chamber before August, 15, 1947. Meanwhile, the Nawab of Bhopal, helped by his stooges like Mr. Maqbool Mahmood continued his activities in organizing the Princes Union in order to dictate their terms for integration to the future Government of India. But they did not succeed. Maqbool Mahmood, after getting a cheque for Rs. 1,25,000 encashed it and left Bhopal secretly by a civil aircraft which he had chartered from Delhi. On his way, he collected another lakh of rupees from the Nawabs of Sachin at Cambay and it was only after his departure that the Government of India and the

Chancellor of the Chamber of Princes came to know about his escape. This amount was taken by Maqbool Mahmood with the ostensible purpose of paying the salaries of the staff of the Chamber, but he never did so and in the end the Nawab of Bhopal had to shell out the amount and pay the employees from his own privy purse. Before Maqbool Mahmood was asked to resign sometime in May 1947, Mr. D.R. Ratnam, I.C.S., was appointed as secretary to the Chancellor to wind up the affairs of this organisation."

"After the Chamber was dissolved, a Negotiating Committee was formed to negotiate with the Government of India with regard to the terms on which the States should integrate. In this committee, Sardar K.M. Pannikar again played an important part as the Prime Minister or Bikaner State. He advised the Maharaja of Bikaner to integrate and his advice was accepted. The second State to integrate was Baroda, whose patriotic Prime Minister, Sir B. L. Mitter, also played a conspicuous part in persuading the Maharaja to integrate with India. After these two premier Indian States had integrated, the other States followed suit and there was no difficulty whatsoever in persuading the rest of the rulers to act similar!"

It is pertinent to point out here that in both these States, Bikaner and Baroda, Diwan Jarmani Das had lot of influence. Their Maharajas and Prime Ministers were his cronies.

Tribute to Mahatma Gandhi and Rebuke to Communalists

When Mahatma Gandhi was assassinated on January 30, 1948 at Birla House, Delhi, Jarmani Dass was invited to address a largely attended public meeting. He had met Mahatma Gandhi many times in his life. Mahatmaji also had a very high regard for him because of his brilliance and love for the motherland. The condolence meeting was held on the February 7, 1948, at the premises of Jamna Hosiery Mills, Turkman Gate, Delhi. It was attended by eminent public figures including Maulana Ahmed Sayeed, Shafa-ul-Mulk Hakim, Dilbar Hassan Khan, Srimati Krishna Dulari, the then Hon. Magistrate at Aligarh, Monsieur Francis Brunnel and others. In the meeting Diwan Sahib castigated the communal parties. He had also a word of advice for the socialist opposition party. His speech was highly emotional. People listened to him with rapt attention. The following is a moving extract from his speech:

"Fellow countrymen and women I cannot be equal to what our leaders have said in the last few days about

Mahatmaji. Kings, Presidents and Prime Ministers of nearly all the countries of the world, poets, writers, industrialists and religious leaders have also paid homage to Mahatmaji by sending messages in his praise. We read this morning in the newspapers that President Truman was attending the memorial service for Mahatma Gandhiji. The whole world is paying homage to Mahatmaji. There is nothing new that I can say about this great saint, philosopher and guide who was born in India to perform a special mission to liberate India and Asia from the foreign yoke. I may, however, pay my homage to Mahatmaji and ask you all to follow his principle. Mahatmaji was as great as Jesus Christ, Mohammad and Buddha. The comparisons are obvious but Mahatmaji was unique in the world history. Mahatmaji's teachings will be remembered for ever and his new religion of non-violence and truth will spread all over the world.

Mahatmaji followed his inner voice to the end of his life. He lead a simple life. His principles were high and correct to the changing times of Indian History. He stuck to his loin-cloth in India and wore the same in the courts and chanceries of Europe. I narrate to you an eyewitness account of Mahatmaji when he was invited to England to attend the second Round Table Conference. There was a reception by King George V and Queen Mary of England at the Royal Buckingham Palace in honour of the Indian delegates to the Round Table Conference. It was mentioned on the invitation card that the guests should come in ceremonial dress. Mahatmaji told the Secretary of State for India that he would go to Buckingham

Palace only in his usual dress which was a loin-cloth a symbol of poverty of teeming millions in India. The Secretary of State informed the King that Gandhiji could come only in his usual dress. The King got annoyed and told the Secretary of State that Gandhi should not be invited. The Secretary of State got in touch with the Viceroy of India on the telephone and informed him what was transpiring. The Viceroy told the Secretary of State that the absence of Gandhiji from the Reception will much be resented by Indians and the function will not have any importance without Gandhiji. He also told the Secretary of State to tell the King to let Gandhiji come in his usual dress. The King then allowed Gandhiji to come in any dress that he liked. Gandhiji told the Secretary of State that he was representing the poor people of India who have no clothes to wear and he being their representative could not come in any other dress than that usually worn by the poorest of Indians. I remember well that when Mahatmaji entered the Reception Hall in the Buckingham Palace all the eyes were focussed on him. Princes, Princesses, Dukes, and Duchesses and members of the diplomatic corps and the elite of the English Society were gazing at him when the King was seen talking to Mahatmaji in an angry tone. What transpired I do not know but next morning at the conference presided over by the Prime Minister of England, Mr. Ramsay Macdonald, Mahatmaji made one of his most brilliant speeches which I have ever heard. Mahatmaji said that some one threatened yesterday, if India did not become loyal to England and if he (Mahatmaji) preached disloyalty to the Crown of England more troops would be sent to India to quell any rebellion. Mahatmaji said that his children in India considered the bullets and bombs as mere crackers to play with. I had the privilege to sit at the same Round Table in front of Mahatmaji for several weeks as a delegate from India. Mahatmaji's parting message to us on January 30 was that we should unite and the Hindus should look to the Muslims as their brethren and vice-versa. We should only save us from complete ruin and tender us prosperous and make our country a powerful one. It was Mahatmaji who raised us from serfdom to freedom. I remember very well that I went around the world for the first time at the age of about 22 years, Indians were treated as savages and slaves. We were not admitted to the clubs, we were not allowed to be put up in the first class hotels. We were treated as people belonging to inferior races. Now by the magic wand of Mahatmaji's hand we can hold our head high and walk in the streets of London, New York and Paris as citizens of a free country. We have our ambassadors in all the countries of the world and our national flag flutters atop our Embassies and our prestige in the world has heightend. Mahatmaji brought this change of status to us. We achieved independence but can we maintain it? We can do so only if we support our present Government and uproot the communal organisations and if all the political parties abandon their activities against the Government. I do not mean to say that there should not be a growth of political parties in this country but this is not the time for them to obstruct the constructive work which the

Government is doing. India's independence is like a new-born baby and we should not kill it by creating communal riots and starting strikes in the country. The socialist party and other political parties which want to indulge in power politics must cease their activities in order that the present Government may have the chance to build India into a powerful country by developing her industries and her vast mineral resources. If we allow the communal organisations and political parties to obstruct the progress of the country. We will be doomed and some other foreign power will conquer us again and our independence will be short lived. We must not forget that foreign powers are just watching us like hawks and will pounce upon us when they find that we are weak, divided and unable to defend ourselves. Can the men and women of this country realise what is in store for us if we do not wake up and support our Government? We have the good fortune to have a great leader in Pandit Jawahar Lal Nehru who should be given full powers to handle the present situation in India. India can safely leave her destiny in his hands.

Now I want to tell something to my Muslim friends. They should not look to Mr. Jinnah or the Pakistan Government for help and protecting. They should live in India as true citizens and forget Pakistan if unfortunately there is a war between Pakistan as enemies. Look at the Muslims in Russia. Will they ever have sympathy for the Muslim of India if ever India was attacked by Russia? The Muslims of Russia, Turkey, Moraca and other Muslim countries consider Muslims of

India as foreign as the Christians of England and America and the some principle should be followed in India. They shauld protect their countrymen if their co-religionist from abroad attack their motherland. I strongly urge the Muslims of this country to give up their moral support to the Muslim League and the Muslim National Guard as I want Hindus and Sikhs to give up their communal organisations so that India becomes one united country and we may preserve our independence which we have obtained after centuries of slavery. The members of these organisations persist in creating communal hatred and violence and foster among the Muslim community extra territorial loyalty.

I ask you, fellow countrymen and women, to stand in complete silence for two minutes to pay homage to Mahatmaji."

How prophetic his words which were uttered even four decades ago. The dissecting analysis and diagnosis is very much relevant to the perilous situation in which the country is engulfed today with monstrous communalism and sectarianism which if not check-mated can spell damnation and doom for the country, forever.

Why He Penned the *Maharaja* – Pied Piper of Indian Princes

Diwan Jarmani Dass's best-seller and world famous book *Maharaja* was published at the most opportune time. The publication of the book was like an explosion. Within days it became known all over the country and after sometime it was being read all over the world. There were requests for translation from different corners of the country. There were proposals for the translation into French, German, etc. The book was discussed in the Parliament and the pulpit. Jarmani Dass as author became famous all over the world in the late 1970. The Maharajas stood exposed fulminated, fretted and fumed. There were some protests from Maharajas and their cronies. Letters of congratulations from the common readers poured in. Many readers expressed surprise and shock on learning about the type of jawed lives the Maharajas had led. Those who knew about the private lives of the Maharajas vouched for the veracity of each line written in the book. His close friend Sardar K.M. Pannikar was afraid that the author would soon be trapped in a string of litigations. He told him that he would soon be garlanded by defamation cases. Stella Mudge, the British Cabaret girl, whose adventures with Paramjit Singh are so widely described in the book, came all the way from London to enter into polemics with Jarmani Dass in Delhi. She frowned upon Jarmani vehemently and burst forth: "Jarmani you have defamed me to the hilt. I am going to drag you to the courts and will launch defamation proceedings against you...." Jarmani Dass retorted humorously, "Lady, you have little realized that by mentioning you in the book you have become immortal, you should thank me on this count." Nothing came out from the threat posed by the Maharajas. He had stood all along like a rock in the face of threats. What gave him the strength was the documentary proof that he had with him of all that he had stated in the book. He had kept a pure leather box in his house whose locks had never been opened by anyone except himself. Inside he had kept clippings from French, Spanish, English and German newspapers, pocket diaries, photos and other original documents. Every incident that he had described in the book was based on facts and the evidence was lying in the mysterious box. When the book was published, a copy was presented to Shri Y.B. Chavan, at that time the Union Home Minister. The photograph of Diwan Jarmani Dass presenting the book was widely published in the country. The princes were afraid of suing him in the court thinking he had the support and backing of the Government of India. Maharani of Jubbul caught hold of the tie of Jarmani Dass at the clinic of Dr. M. L. Soni, renowned dentist, at his Golf Link clinic in Delhi and reprimanded him for daring to write such a book. Diwan replied that Maharani Sahiba she should wait for the book *Maharani* where the private lives of Maharanis will be revealed.

Most of the Princes had signed the Instrument of Accession knowing fully well that there was no way out. Their own people, headed by Praja Mandals, were at their throat. In lieu of the "sovereignty" they had wangled many privileges. Apart from fat privy purses, privileges, etc. they had lucrative jobs. Many had been accepted as "Leaders" in the ruling party itself. When half of abolition of privy purses was in the air, the princes tried their best to stall it. In the Swatantra Party, they found a political platform. They approached the world court to stall the move. The adventurous among them talked of even re-establishing "Princestan" (Land of Princes).

Such were the times when *Maharaja* was published. The book gave a terrible blow to the feudal and reactionary elements. It strengthened the hands of Indira Gandhi, Y. B. Chavan and other Congress leaders who wanted to abolish the privy purses. After publication of the book, the Princes seldom talked of their "past glory". The book further proved to be a coup-de-grace to the princely order.

The ancestors of Diwan Jarmani Dass had faithfully served the royal house of Kapurthala. His father, grandfather and great-grandfather were ministers in the same State. Maharaja Jagjit Singh owned his throne to Diwan Ramjas. It was his planning which had placed a Chopra Khatri child on the Gadi of an Ahluwalia Sikh State. Diwan Ramjas had done so to keep away the rightful claimant that is the family of Late Raj Kumari Amrit Kaur, the first Health Minister of India, who had renounced her Sikh faith and embraced Christianity to please the British imperialists. Maharaja Jagjit Singh owned his gratitude to the family and treated Jarmani Dass with love and care. Maharaja Bhupinder Singh of Patiala was also very close to him and treated him with utmost courtesy and respect. Many other princes were also very friendly with the question that naturally comes to the mind of the readers of *Maharaja* is, therefore: Why the author wrote about Princes so viciously? His son Parmajit's affairs with British Cabaret star Stella are too well known to be mentioned. He was Pandit Nehru's classmate at Harrow. He used to carry a dozen precious watches on his purse and move about with a fancy walking stick even as a student. Maharaja Bhupinder Singh of Patiala had 326 wives.

Many of them did not have even the privilege of being caressed by the Maharaja Yadavinder Singh of Patiala and hatched an intrigue against Diwan Jarmani Dass by asking his confidants to forge a letter and get signature of Diwan Sahib.

The other thing that prompted him to write the book was that the princes were all stooges of British whereas he himself was a staunch nationalist to the core. At a very early age he came under the influence of the nationalists. Jarmani Dass joined the Congress in 1917. His elder brother, Chief Justice of Kapurthala Diwan Sureshwer Dass, was a revolutionary who wrote the book *Joys and Sorrows of India* on account of which he was shadowed by the British Intelligence all his life. His name was also lined with Harding Bomb conspiracy at Delhi. Jarmani Dass helped the Praja Mandal movement in Kapurthala in all respects. His ancestral house, Red House, was the favourite rendezvous and hide out of the underground nationalists where revolutionaries like Bhai Parmanand and Lala Hardial etc. used to stay and feel safe from eyes of the British. A conflict between him and the Maharajas was, therefore, inevitable.

The book was very widely reviewed in the media both in India and abroad. He was interviewed by press representatives in India and Europe. The German correspondent of Der Spiegel carried his interview story. Letters started pouring in to him from Germany. Mr. H. Reinautz an old friend from Munich, wrote that as a result of his book the Princes would probably lose their privy purses. This prophecy came true. He was sent a reply which satisfied him.

As his reputation as an author spread, he started receiving offers of collaboration from the leading writers of the world. One American author, Mr. Humpry Evens, sought his collaboration for writing a book on India. Jarmani Dass wrote back that he would not collaborate in writing a book that depicted India in a bad light even if he was offered fabulous remuneration. Original letters are available in his personal records which show that he spurned many such offers from writers and publishers.

Maharaja is not merely a mirror through which one sees with lividness the lewd lives of Indian Princes but the discerning readers hardly fail to notice the poetic luster of his expression, the artistic bent of his mind and the intrinsic harmony he had ceaselessly endeavoured to achieve all of which make us think that some new classics are added to the treasury of English language and literature. Nay, he had laid bare the conflicts of his mind, the tensions of the heart all the urges, aspirations and travails of his generations. He has surveyed the world as a humanist and has attracted the teeming millions all over the world to hear him as if he were the "flute of Krishna" or the Pied Piper of Hamelin.

Champion of Tourism

In 1950, Jarmani Dass conceived an idea that in order to earn valuable foreign exchange, tourism should be promoted. Thereby he sent a comprehensive scheme to Pt. Jawaharlal Nehru. He had many times advised the Minister in charge of Tourism at the Centre to bring out colourful and high quality publications throwing light on our holy places for the benefits of scholarly tourists who had a philosophical bent of mind. The literature brought out by the tourism officials lacked profundity. He himself, therefore, wrote down a pamphlet which became a trail blazer. In September 1958 he visited the holy shrines of Badrinath with the company of his wife. Before going there they took the blessing of Swami Sivananda of Rishikesh. Mr. H. Hess, and Mrs. Margaret Hess, Mrs. Eric Metha of the Swiss Embassy and Mr. and Mrs. Lola D. Fowler. Dr. H. Hess, the then Ambassador of Switzerland in India and Dr. Bernhelin, Journalist accompanied the party up to Srinagar in Tehri Garwal, U.P. The exquisite beauty, scenic setting and the *mise-en-scene* of this marvellous temple find their eloquent expression in the ensuing narrative of Diwan Sahib.

"Badrinath is the most important sacred Dhama (sacred place) among four Dhams of Bharatversam and is the abode of Shri Badrinarayanan, one of the many incarnations of God Vishnu, incarnated in the form of Nar Narayan. It is situated on the right bank of the river Alaknanda on a plain surface on the Pauri Garhwal outflanking on the eastern border of Tibet at a height of 10,500 feet from the sea level, with Thermal Spring at 122 feet close to it and the snow-clad mountains hanging over it. The Puranic name of this part of the country is Kedarkhand. It comprises the area from Pindari Glaciers in the east to Jamna glaciers in the west and from the Ganga Maidan or Alkapuri in the north to Mayapuri (Haridwar) in the South."

"Badrinath was a religious place during and long before the Mahabharata era. It suffered eclipse when Buddhism was on the ascendance. It was again renewed by the Adi Shankaracharya in the seventh century. It is also called Badrikashram where Lord Vishnu performed penance."

"From Haridwar to Badrinath we followed the gigantic Ganges surrounded by beautiful thick deodar and pine trees and multicoloured flower gardens and colourful crop plant right up to Badrinath. The rivers Bhagirathi and Alaknanda form the great Ganges which flow over vast regions to the other end of India and merges in the Bay of Bengal. The roaring sound of the river coming as it does from the highest and loftiest mountains of Himalayans and the icy water of Ganges coming in terrific speed prevented and surpassed now and then by huge stones and surrounded by gigantic and magnificent mountains clad in snow inspired feelings of serenity."

"Here the solemn majesty of the great Himalayas breathes a magnificent sense of grandeur; where from rock to rock cataracts cascade; the thunder crashes and the lightening flashes; amidst the musical sound of the running brooks and rills and water falls."

As to Pandit Nehru so to Diwan Sahib "Himalayas seem calm and inscrutable with all the wisdom of past ages, might of them cooled the fever in the brain and the petty conflicts and intrigues, the lusts and falsehoods of the plains and the city seemed trivial and far away before their eternal ways."

He prepared a pamphlet to mobilise public opinion and drew the attention of the Government towards the need for boosting foreign tourist traffic. He had gone around the world many times and had mixed with the aristocracy of his times in the leading cities of Europe and America. As such none knew more than him the difficulties the foreign tourist faced in India than him. While he was appalled at the ignorance of the foreigners about the Indian heritage, he also at the same time appreciated their difficulties. He wanted to clarify the dubious impressions created by the British that India is a land of snake-charmers, rope-dancers, jugglers, oil-rubbers, etc. In those days Catherine Mayo's book *Mother India* was avidly read in Europe while it was condemned in India. He planned to give a fitting reply to such authors and at the same time wanted to help the genuine tourists in understanding the country. He proposed the setting up of an information bureau under Bharat Sadhu Samaj of which he was the Chairman of Delhi Metropolis chapter to provide information to the tourists seeking to see places associated with religions and satisfy their spiritual quest. He wanted a training course for guides and tourists and literature prepared by learned men. All holy places should have accommodation fit for tourists. He underlined the need for friends of Indian societies in foreign countries under the patronage of our embassies. He himself had a sound knowledge of Indian philosophy, arts and other ancient attainments typifying the hoary history of India.

In a highly scholastic and philosophic view he sings panegyries to the rich treasure-chest of Indian thought, idiom and ideology when he pens:

"It should be pointed out here that the philosophical study in the Medieval times was later applied to practical arts, and physio-spiritual theories of India in ancient times were described in religious treaties, and these theories were expounded in the Samkhya-Patanjali and Nyaaya Vaiseshika system of Hindu philosophy."

"According to Dr. P. Ray the Vedantic view of the evolution of matter, the atomic theory of Buddhists and Jains, the chemical theory of Nyaaya Vaiseshika system, including Kanad's view of the Nyaaya Vaiseshika system, including Kanad's view of the nature of atoms and moledules and their combination, the theory of light, heat, combustion and molecules, had all been dealt extensively in Hindu philosophy. The theory of the sound had been described in Mimansas and Chemistry of digestion in the treaties of Charka and Bagbhata. The theory of heredity has been unfolded by Charka and Aarey. The conception of life as advocated by Charka has been widely approved. Knowledge of metallurgical processes, metallic salts, alloys and amalgams was very extensive. Traces of copper and iron found in large quantities at Taxila in 1943-45 show that India was much advanced in metallurgy even in the third century B.C."

"The metallic finds including household utensils, arms besides tools for carpenters, blacksmiths and agricultural implements, iron clamps found at the Bodh Gaya Temple furnish evidence of the manufacture of iron as early as the third century B. C. The iron pillar of Delhi is an outstanding example of highly advanced metallurgical processes. This was moulded in the fourth century A.D."

The aforementioned observations of Jarmani Dass are replete with philosophical profundity, scholastic insight and erudition of high order.

Attitude towards Women

> "Dear Jarmani, if you are successful with women, you are successful in Life."
>
> **Sir Sultan Mohamed Shah**
>
> The Agha Khan III, 1923

His Highness the Agha Khan, grandfather of Prince Karim, the present Agha Khan told him when he was barely 30 years old and was his guest at the Savoy Hotel, London, at a diner party given by him to which he had also invited Mr. Edwin Montague, the Secretary of State for India and many other prominent personalities, after he danced a tango with Princess Andress Caroon Agha Khan, his French consort and one of the most beautiful and cultured women of her time: "Jarmani as (he used to call him in familiar tone), if you are successful with women, you are successful in life."

This advice by the Agha Khan, though given in a jocular manner and in a jolly mood, went home, and all his life he made efforts to become friendly with Maharanis, princesses and other women in all walks of life. Besides giving him happiness, his friendship with them paid him rich dividends. All his life he was helped and favoured by women not only in India but throughout the world. He became intimate with women of several nationalities in different parts of the world. Wherever he went he always made it a point to cultivate the friendship of women.

He has written in his book *Maharani* that in Paris where he spent the greater part of his youth and middle age, visiting Maharanis and Princesses every evening, he had 20 to 25 women, including foreign women of aristocracy, to choose from but he did not confine himself to high society alone. He has equally keen to meet girls selling flowers in the streets and shop girls. He was very successful even with this class of girls.

For an observer of life and reader of *Maharaja* Jarmani Dass was a lady killer par excellence and essentially a women's man. He had to mix with extra smart Indian and foreign women because his profession dictated him to do so. He was duty bound to mix with them. He could not avoid Princesses and wives and daughters of Kings, Emperors, Dukes and Dictators. In his heart of heart he was an orthodox man who firmly believed that the right place for a woman was her home and the right duty was to make home a happy home. He had gone around the world and mixed with the women of many nationalities. After all this experience he came to the conclusion that there was nothing in the world compared to Indian woman. They were paragons of virtue and matchless in beauty and grace. He did not hesitate to express his views about Indian women even when he and Maharaja Jagjit Singh were mobbed by American beauties and blondes in New York. The following report published in the New York Evening Journal of October 4, 1929 throws light on his views on women.

"The faces of both the Maharaja and his aide brightened."

"If progress may be reckoned by achievement, then our women are the most progressive in the world, and I believe that the time will come when they will be leaders."

"They have achieved everything that occidental women desire and have already achieved. They are eligible to be in parliament. They are brilliant, happy, highly educated, great workers in politics and social reforms and are the equal of any women of any race in the world."

"My own wife is an example." added Sardar Dass. He produced pictures of a young worn in sari, whose beauty and spirit might attract Florenza Ziegfeld. Slender, radiant and keenly alive, her face looks out from every available corner of Sardar Jarmani Dass's room.

"And the daughter of His Highness, who is married to the reigning Prince of Mandi, is another worker in all public causes. Her Highness and my wife are typical of our womanhood. I don't think an occidental would find them any different from his own save, perhaps, that they are naturally a little more shy and simple in their tastes. But you remember that they have been responsible for a wonderful change, under the auspices of such progressive Princes as Her Highness."

He believed that it was the influence of the British residing in India and the deliberate policy of the British Government in the 20th century that brought about a complete change in the character of Maharajas, Princesses, and women in the high strata of society. The so-called emancipation of women and the so-called modern education imparted to the women in India, offering them high positions not only in the Government but also in commerce and industry, in the Army, Navy, Air Force and other departments of administration engendered a mental climate which adversely governed their social ways, and values.

He talked to many of his friends in high society about this and most of them admit that due to preoccupation with politics, social life and travels abroad their wives had completely lost touch with their homes, husbands and children. A case he used to quote related to a sensational report submitted by Mr. M.M. Basu, Chief Secretary of the West Bengal Government. The reports runs as follows:

"Mr. Raghunath Banerjee, Joint Secretary and Commissioner of the Presidency Division and Special Officer of Indo-Pak boundary in Bengal, had in a short period illegitimate and immoral connections with 50 women whom he enticed to his bed by offers of employment, increment and promotion. He was prematurely retired for indulging in sex orgies in his air-conditioned office room furnished with a sofa set and a dressing table at the State expense." Jarmani Dass thought of, one Joint Secretary could entice 50 married and unmarried women to his bed, how many thousands, the secretaries and other officials in Government of the States must be entering the pattern of licentious living."

Happiness in the family can be assured, he believed, only if there were two spheres, one to be controlled by men and the other by women. How happy a home could be if women made that home comfortable, beautiful and hospitable and looked after the development of their children who were the future citizens of India? He wrote of the ideal home as follows :

"Formerly, men worked in the fields, fought in wars and undertook hazardous jobs and performed their duties more efficiently than today. These days men go back home only to find their wives away or busy in offices and in some case on official tour in India and abroad. Finding themselves in utter loneliness they try to find solace in the company of other women. This disrupts society on the whole and at the base. The efficiency of husband and the well-being of children depend on the comforts and care they get at home. What a beautiful home it is where the wife is devoted to her husband and children!"

He did not like the way the Women's Liberation movement was going on in India. He wanted traditions to be respected. He expresses his views on the subject of current concern in the following words:

"Women spend more money on luxuries now and they consider it their legitimate right to do so. The culture of modern women is how much money and jewellery she possesses and how her house is run luxuriously and what beautiful furniture is in her house. It is this culture which is apparent to the outside world encountered by them. The former idea of spending money on pilgrimage, on charity and giving alms to the poor has vanished from the modern women of India. Though they realise that the way of life that they are leading is not good for the country yet they dislike the idea of going back and initiate the life led by their mother and grandmother." He wanted to modify the life style in a moderate way and not plunge headlong into the quagmire of western mumbo-jumbo of culture and permissiveness.

He did not want the old Hindu joint family system to break. He knew of bureaucrats – petty and big who flirted with their office mates while their wives languished at home. This made him a bitter critic of the so-called women's emancipation. Similarly, he did not like the middle class habit of attaching a stigma to a girl who came from a poor family. To such persons he used to tell the history of the slave markets of Middle East. One such historical fact he used to tell makes interesting reading:

"In Baghdad and in Istanbul girls were sold naked in the market, but some of them became Empresses. After being bought, some of them had compensation of their status; the mother of the Abbasid Khallifa Mansur was a barber slave. The famous Khayzursh, mother of Haroon-al-Rasid was also a foreign slave purchased from the slave market. These women ended as Empresses."

He had been to Europe on numerous occasions and understood the European culture, manners more than anyone else. The European society of those times was a decadent society. He felt hurt when he saw the women of India spring the West. In his inimitable style he laments:

"It seems to be our destiny to wear the caste off clothes of Europe. Women of India have been held very high in respect. Compare our tradition with those of the West, he used to say and cite some examples. Only one would suffice here. According to Herodotus every woman amongst the Assyrians and Babylonians was obliged to resort to prostitution once in her life-time in the temples of the Gods – Mylitta, Aphrodite of the Greek. Compare this with the life of women in India during the Vedic age. They enjoyed equal freedom with men. Marriage was simple and widow re-marriage was permitted. There were great scholars among women who were held in high esteem."

Ever since he read *'Todd's Annals and Antiquities of Rajasthan'*, he had become an admirer of Rajputs. Diwan Sahib was well-acquainted with the history of Rajasthan replete with the deeds of bravery, chivalry, gallantry and heroism unmatched in the annals of Indian history. He had read good deal of mythology as well. He realised that the Rajput character never glistened better and brighter than during the Mughal period. They fought invaders valiantly and when they lost in the field their women preferred to commit Sati (Self-immolation) than to fall into the hands of marauders. There is no doubt if the brave and pious women had fallen into the hands of the invaders they would have been dishonoured and sold in the slave markets of Central Asia. He traced the origin of the custom and described in detail the important Johar incidents of history. As early as in 1960 he wrote against the custom which he believed had no relevance in the modern times. While he had the highest regard for the valiant Hindu women who preferred death to dishonour, he strived hard through his writings to stop its practice. He enumerated a few incidents to depict the valiant character of Hindu women of Mughal India. One incident relates to the immolation of 14,000 Rajput women at Chittor – the fortress town of Rajasthan from where the pious men and women bring ash to smear their foreheads with. When Jaswant Singh Rathore lost his battle against Aurangzeb he retreated towards the castle. He was reproached by the Maharani who happened to be the daughter of the Maharana of Mewar for running away from the battlefield. A French writer and traveller Monsieur Buerincin was a witness to the scene. The Rana was killed in the battlefield and the Rani became a Sati for which she had already prepared her mental make-up.

His depiction of such events shows that while he wanted the Sati tradition to be abolished did not approve of people showing disrespect to the great Hindu women of the Mughal period who preferred death to dishonour.

He was against excessive use of make-up. In this connection he used to cite the example of Britain where a law had to be passed against the use of scent and paint. The British Parliament had to pass an Act in 1770 banning the use of scent, paints and other such artificial means to enhance beauty. The British act said :

"That women of whatever age, rank, profession or degree, whether virgin maids or widows that shall from and after such Act impose upon, seduce and betray with matrimony any of His Majesty's subjects by the scent, paints or other such artificial means shall incur the penalty of the law in force against witch-craft and like such misdemeanous and that the marriage upon such convictions should be null and void."

His Business Houses

When he was working in the Censor Department at Bombay, he was offered a high rank in the Army. It had been decided that in the Censor Department noone except the Commissioned Army Officers could work. However he held the title given by H.H. Maharaja of Patiala, Major Jarmani Dass as he was also his military secretary. Jarmani Dass, however, refused to join uniformed service. He was at that time interested in being an ambassador abroad, a post which he could not get. He, therefore, agreed to become the Director in charge of messars. Saksaria Trading Company started by Seth Govind Ram Saksaria of Jaipur, the Cotton King of India in the U.S.A. with a capital of Rs. 25 lakhs. He was stationed at Delhi where he could carry of his other activities as well. This company which had its allies Saksaria Printing Press flourished under his guidance. He was also Director of the Dry Ice Refrigerators Limited, (one of the concerns of Mesar. Karam Chand Thapar and Brothers Ltd., of Calcutta), Chairman of Sun Rise Pictures, Director, Indian Printers Ltd., (Bombay) and Director in charge of Jamna Hosiery Mills Ltd. (Delhi).

His friends made full use of his presence in Delhi and he helped solving several of their problems. For instance, when the Maharaja of Mysore died in 1940 many of Diwan Sahib's bills remained unpaid. The considerable correspondence available shows that at the instances of Yuvraja K. N. R. Wadiyar and Sir Mirza Ismail, the work (whatever it was) done by the Viceroy, Lord Linlithgow at the instance of Diwan Jarmani Dass. He also arranged that Yuvraj's problems were solved by the Viceeroy, Lord Linlithgow, at the recommendation of Lord Glance, Governor of Punjab. Later on when the Congress leaders were associated with the Central Government he offered to relinquish his business interests and serve in the Tourism Department, All India Radio or as a Diplomat in the External Affairs Ministry. Unfortunately he did not have the opportunity to serve the Central Government as an official.

Last Days

On 30 August, 1971, Jarmani Dass went in to eternal sleep. When the doctors asked his wife about how his mortal body was to be prepared and embalmed, etc, she replied it should be done as is done to V.I.P.'s. At the Bombay airport his body was also seen of by Sh. Kabir Bedi. The news of his passing away was flashed by the newspapers the next morning. His coffin was brought to Delhi. Surprisingly thousands had gathered to pay homage to the departed soul at the Palam Airport. Later the mourners joined the funeral to the Electric Crematorium as per the wishes of the late Jarmani Dass.

The news of Diwan Sahibs death spread like wild fire. Condolence messages started pouring in from all over the world. Rich tributes were paid to him by the national press including Hindustan Times, The Times of India, The Indian Express, Nav Bharat Times, etc. As Ex-President of Alliance Francaise de Delhi and its founding committee member, the French community expressed their sadness. He was a champion in promoting Indo-French cultural relations in Delhi.

Nobody had done so much to promote Indo-French friendship as Diwan Sahib and done. There was, therefore, a flood of telegrams from France. Among the prominent Frenchmen who sent condolence telegrams were Jean-Charles Robhr, Deputy Commercial Counsellor, Embassy of France, F. Geoffroy De Chaume, Minister Counsellor, P. Fusche Alliance Francaise De Delhi and M. Veillet-Lavallee and J Lamy of Banque Nationale De Paris. The last mentioned described Diwan Sahib as "An outstanding Indian who has been throughout his life a staunch friend of France." Resolutions condoling his death were passed all over the country. Men and women from all walks of life came to his house for paying homage to his memory. M. Francis wired from Cannes, Kamal Khosla from Addis Ababa, Shri Rajeshwar Barod from Kathmandu, T.R. Khanna from Chicago, His contemporaries such as M.S. Oberoi, (Sir) Sobha Singh, Mrs. Lilawati, Mrs. Elizabeth Reid of Afpro were grief-stricken. Swami Hari Nayayanand, Mrs. C.N. Chandra, Miss Surinder Saini, Sarla, Kamla, Gen Shah Nawaz Khan, Shir V.C. Shulka, Union State Home Minister came to pay their respects to his memory. Justice Jagjit Singh of Delhi High Court, Diwan Peyerai, Piare Lal Bedi, his childhood friend and a scholar, M.S. Swaminathan, India's leading Agricultural Scientist, B.P. Pal, Scientist and author, Prof. J. Filliozat, Mrs. S. Aryan, D.N. Malhotra, Mrs. K. Shahzaman, etc. paid rich tributes to his multifaceted personality.

Some Glimpses of His Many Splendoured Personality

Jarmani Dass gave alms and charity to the needy regardless of their religion beliefs. He never hesitated to help his near and dear ones. When a close relative of his asked for a gift on the occasion of a marriage, he gifted cash or kind according to his/her wishes. When the Bhoodan movement picked up in Punjab, landlords in the rural areas of Punjab started giving small tracts of land of inferior quality. Being a true votary of this movement, he surprised every body by giving away 25 acres of highly fertile land at Sultanpur Lodhi, Punjab, which was giving him substantial revenue. His principle was that he would part with this item – may it be cash or in kind – and his visitors and guests should be entertained according to his status. He entertained his guests in a royal fashion. There was no distinction between his servants and himself in matter of food. He never forgot them on happy occasions or at festivals. He shared their joys and sorrows. This is one reason why his servants like Pancham from Bihar, Abdul Majid from Uttar Pradesh, Rehme Khan from Lahore, Daulat Ram and

Chanda Singh were always ready to lay down their lives for him. He won the loyalty of all those who worked under him because he was kind, considerate and benevolent towards them. When a subordinate of his, such as Arjan Dass Bansal, a Superintendent in one of his departments was arrested on false charges in Patiala, he took up his case as his own.

As mentioned earlier, he was very magnanimous even in parting with his huge property. He gave his share from the ancestral properties at Kapurthala which had been used as a shelter by the revolutionaries of the pre-independence era, to his relations, Shrimati Savitri Devi wife of Diwan Wilayati Ram. He gifted his share of majestic Haveli to Diwan Mankeshar Dass his youngest brother Madan Lal and Rameshwar Dass, sons of his eldest brother Sureshwar Dass who was prior to his demise Chief Justice and Home Minister of Kapurthala State. He gave a big tract of fertile land to he Munshi Gurdita Mal and another tract of land at Sultanpur Lodhi to his driver Chanda Singh at Gilla village. He gave cash to his faithful servant Rehma Nai, who went off to Lahore.

Ministers and courtiers of those days used to amass wealth by pleasing the Rajas and Maharajas by one way or the other. In this respect he was an unusual man. He had served under Maharaja Jagjit Sing of Kapurthala a reasonably rich State of India. He could ask him for anything but he did not. Similarly, when in his service, Maharaja Bhupinder Singh asked him to pick up anything that he liked from a famous Jewellery Shop in Paris, he picked up a small imitation of ivory box with chord of animals. When a similar offer was made to others, they picked up diamond-studded jewellery or other precious stones. When he defeated Maharaja Bhupinder Singh in chess he declined to take the money that he had won. At the persistence of the Maharaja, he asked for a cheque for one anna. This cheque is displayed in his house. He always gave his advice to the Maharaja openly and freely and worked for the interest of the State. He was unmindful of his personal interest. Maharaja Bhupinder Singh of Patiala held him in high regard. He had declared that in his State the word of Jarmani Dass should carry as much weight as his own words. As Minister-in-Charge of Health and the Palace, Jarmani Dass had been given the authority to accompany the famous French Gynecologist Dr. Joseph Dore from Paris in 1936 on his round examining the Ranis and Maharanis for their ailments. He used to be the only person present even when the ladies were examined internally. Maharaja Bhupinder Singh always consulted him in selecting brides and grooms for his children. The great Maharaja loved to establish matrimonial relationships with the leading Rajput princes of India. Bigoty ever entered his mind. However, Prince Yadavinder Singh was most unlike him. The father loved women but the son was a misogynist. Otherwise also Yadavinder Singh was poles apart from his father in thinking. Jarmani and Maharaja Bhupinder Singh had got him married to a beautiful Rajput princess of Patna (Bihar). Prince Yadavinder being a staunch Sikh never had marital relations with her. He married Mehtab Kaur, after his father's death, daughter of Haricharan Singh Jaji who had earlier been exiled from the State. Jarmani Dass was never afraid of giving saner counsels and advice even on such sensitive matters.

It is a sheer delight to read his handwritten letters and diaries maintained by him in his early days. He used holders and nibs with which he could draw extremely light *serifs* of alphabet. He could thicken the nib whenever he wanted. The result was that his handwriting has exemplary. When he wrote Persian couplets he used a different medium. The result was that his Persian was a pleasure to read. Towards the latter part of his life, his handwriting deteriorated as usual. As far as Urdu is concerned he continued to write in the same style till the end.

While he was very lavish in spending his own money, he thought twice before spending public money. Maharaja Jagjit Singh had always treated him as his son and given him authority to spend on whatever he thought was essential. In spite of this blanket permission he never wasted a penny out of State funds. His diary written in 1920 makes very interesting study. When he gave a tip to the waiter or threw a coin into sea before boarding the ship he made an entry in the diary. Even alms given to the beggars were noted and each page of the diary was signed. When he came hack from journeys to far-flung countries, he gave these authenticated accounts to the concerned department of the State.

He had evolved a method of naming his near and dear

ones and servants. He called his wife. L.H. (Light of Heart) who in turn called him L.H (Loving Husband) A servant of his who was stupid was named B.K. (Bewakoof). The ailment from which he suffered was cancer but he called it Captain because he did not want to reveal that he was ill. He thought people would unnecessarily pour in to enquire about his health. Even when he was suffering from acute pain he used to get up to receive the guests. The best way, therefore, was to keep the illness secret.

He maintained the record of his meetings with personages such as Benito Mussolini, Clemenceau, Ramsay Macdonald, Hirohito, Haile Selassie, Sultan of Turkey etc. He also preserved important letters which have great historical value today. But the thing of the greatest delight to the research scholars are the numerous newspapers in English, French and Spanish which throw a flood of light on the epoch-making events of the early 30th century. Such papers used to be dumped hy him in a big leather box. Whenever his wife expressed a desire to know what was in the box he would say "Let it remain a mystery". These papers now reveal that every word that he wrote his famous book 'Maharaja' is based on facts. The innumerable photographs of the bygone age are a veritable treasure-trove for a scholar or a film maker. Some of the newspapers are as old as 80 years.

He had spent most of his time in the company of the Maharajas. The food used to be most delicious but rich and heavy. While in Europe he ate in the world's best hotels in the company of the elite of Europe. Even there in his heart of hearts he yearned for the home cooked food with a typical Punjabi flavour. At the first available opportunity he would rush home and ask for a simple meal which normally consisted of curd, vegetable, dal and meat. He relished the simple dal-roti cooked in Punjabi fashion than the world's best treats. His favourites were potatoes, chana dal, peas, cauliflower, non-vegetarian dishes, and *laddus*.

Patiala is known even to this dal for its (large) peg called in popular Pepsu parlance as Patiala Peg. A person's status in the olden days at Patiala was determined by his alcohol bill. Those with exorbitantly high bills were considered rich and manly. He consumed it in a moderate fashion, limit was two small pegs in company, or social parties made no difference to him.

He shared his joys with other but no sorrows. He never shared his mental anguish with others. When he was critically ill with cancer of back-bone and suffered from shooting pain, he calmly lay down on his bed. He even did not wake up his wife at night to help him.

He believed his life as a Yagna. He was born to serve and help others for all times to come. His loyalty and sincerity did not diminish with time of when out of sight. Even after leaving the service of the Maharaja of Kapurthala he helped him whenever he asked for it. Whenever the Maharaja or his Princes sought an audience with the Viceroy, they approached him. Knowing Diwan Jarmani Dass was always close to the Viceroys, it was not difficult for him to get the interviews for the Princes. Even when he was himself in adversity, he helped his friends. He would never talk ill of his relatives, friends or foes behind their back. He did not like people who made political somersaults for personal gains. He always preached his associates to compare his plus points with his minus points. He wanted them to leave the minus points and adopt the plus points. He believed no man is fully negative. He was straight-forward in his dealings and consistent with his political views. Diwan Dina Nath was the Diwan of Indore State who always dressed in Western style.

He had likes and dislikes for people in his life but seldom gave expression to his views. He was diplomatic in his conversation with such persons so much so that they could never imagine they were not liked by him. He called some persons traitors. For this word, the acronym was TT. After a person had left he would warn his wife to be aware of him. He had always carried his point. He was a hard task master in his office and at home. He was a democrat. At the same time he stood to reason.

He prayed daily before a photograph of Guru Nanak Sahib ji. He performed pujas and observed other rituals of the orthodox Hindus. He helped the Sadhus, Saints and Fakirs in a lavish maner. He had great faith in Bible. His retinue of servants hailed from all religions and there used to be about a dozen of them on full time basis. His favourite servant was Rehma Barbar who used to massage him daily. There are letters in his record room from Muslim notables thanking him for his donation to mosques. He often attended the Nizamuddin, on VIP pass. Such letter is from "Institute-de-Muslim" Paris written during the twenties. There was an Arya Samaji Swami Diwan Chand Verma who resided at Paris and became his friend and admirer in the early twenties. It is the same Swami who performed his marriage with Laila after converting her to Hindu faith. Later on this Swami shifted to U.K. at 11 Wellington Court, Knights Bridge, S.W.I. London where probably now his descendants live.

He was a well of wit and witticism. He could entertain his guests with most appropriate jokes and incidents from his experience to enliven the atmosphere. Being an intellectual and a polyglot, he freely quoted from as diverse sources as Voltaire and Burke to Sa'adi (a Persian poet) and Nanak. On 1 April, it gave him pleasure to make fool of others. When somebody sent him a telegram that the Maharaja of Dholpur was eager to have a talk with him regarding his vote for Maharaja Bhupinder Singh for election to Chancellor of Chamber of Princes, he quickly borrowed the personal plane of the Maharaja and reached Bikaner. On arrival, there on the first April, he found that he had been befooled. He took it most sportingly. A day before his death, he was cutting jokes with the doctor attending him at Tata Memorial, Bombay.

He was a great admirer of Nehru whom he knew since very early days. His other favourite was Sarojini Naidu. Mahatma Gandhi was of course like an apostle to him. He had high regards for brilliant persons like Prime Ministers of various States like LiaHuat Hayat Khan, Sir Mirza Ismail,

Sardar K.M. Pannikar and eminent jurists. He had very high regard for H.H. the Agha Khan-III. He revered him like his father. He valued his friendship with Jinnah who also held him in high regard.

He helped many men to rise in life. Among such men who rose to become famous in the world were Prithvi Raj Kapur, Pt. Uday Shankar and Devika Rani. He helped them with advice and his contacts. Prithvi Raj and Uday Shankar expressed their thanks many times to him. Similarly he helped numerous other people to rise in life. However, he never made a show of it nor did he expect any return for it.

His personality won him admires in many countries. One such admirer was Mr. Kaye who included his name in the World Biography. The Institute for Research in Biography, Bethpage, New York are the publishers of the Biographical Encyclopedia of the World which is an authentic record of noted living men and women in every country throughout the world. The fifth edition of this encyclopedia published the biography of Diwan Jarmani Dass. For this the Editor Mr. S.A. Kaye persuaded him to supply the details and go through the machine proofs. His name with a small note on his life was listed in the book's "Who's & Who."

He had a thorough command over many languages including English, Persian, Urdu, German, but as far as French is concerned, he spoke it as the French. He had joined the University at Sorbonne, France and stayed with a French family at Paris during his first visit to that city.

Within six months he began to follow the lectures on political economy at the University. When he returned to India in 1917, Maharaja Jagjit Singh felt very impressed that he could speak French fluently and appointed him Deputy Director of Education. He remained in this post for two years. He soon rose to the position of Military Secretary at the age of 27 and after two years was elevated to the post of a Minister. Initially it was his command over Tennis and the languages that impressed Maharaja Jagjit Singh the most. He was very fond of hosting lavish parties at home. Miss Paramjyoti, a teacher of French and Art at St. Columbus remembers how with great easily he could switch over from one language to the other. His French had literary flair.

He was a good tennis player of his times. As a matter of fact, the Maharaja of Kapurthala, Jagjit Singh was fascinated by his game. He had won the Single's Championship of the University of Punjab by beating the best tennis player of the University of Punjab whose name was Sunder Das Sood, a student of the Government College, Lahore. Sunder Das had later became the Cambridge Blue in Tennis and was known as the best player of Punjab at that time. The Maharaja was so pleased with his victory in winning the championship, that in an open investiture ceremony he pinned on his chest, with his own hand, a gold medal with the inscription "Champion of the Punjab University" offered by His Highness Maharaja Jagjit Singh of Kapurthala. In this game Jarmani Dass was declared Champion of

Phulkian State after he defeated the leading players in matches. He was also declared Champion of Chateau., De Goia, Pranch. The other game in which he excelled was hockey played on skates. Later on Patiala became famous for this game because of his efforts. Even when he was a student in France, he won many sports events. He was a good rider himself and he encouraged riding during his service in Kapurthala and Patiala States. His brown riding books from London are still preserved as memory. He won many medals in equestrian competitions. Because of his fondness for these games, his body was stronger and muscular. He had a mastery over such indoor games as ping-pong, chess, bridge, etc.

He launched a vigorous campaign against the evil of dowry system and the useless expenditure incurred on pomp and pageantry at the time of marriage. He prepared a draft act containing 27 points and a pamphlet attacking this social evil. This was widely distributed to mobilise public opinion. The current Act bears resemblance of his draft but unfortunately he did not live to see the Act that has been passed by the parliament. In this pamphlet he traces the origin of the system, its evil effect the society and explains how it ultimately works against the interest of all especially women. He believed that this evil could be eradicated only by the enactment of a law because earlier attempts by various baradaries (fraternities) had failed to yield any result. His draft act had 27 articles. One of these articles exhorts the Government to appoint Dowry Control Officers in each district to enforce this law with the assistance of Inspectors and Wardens.

From his first Childhood marriage with Bibi Kam Kandla, Jarmani Dass had got a daughter named Brij Kishori. It was later Laila, an Egyptian and Sushila. Bibi Kam Kandla was very handsomely provided for at the time of separation. She started living at Dehra Dun where Jarmani Dass provided her ancestral jewellery, household effects, a monthly pension with a villa along with an orchard. From Sushila Devi a son, Rakesh Bhan Dass, was born in 1947.

Though "Dhir" was the surname of the Diwan Ramjas family, it was only used by present generation only.

Diwan Sahib, Sushila and Rakesh became the disciples of Swami Purushotamji of Vashisht Gufa the village near Goolar Dogi, Dist. Tehri Garhwal 20 km up from Rishi Vaishistha Gufa, has a history of many past Saghas, Swamis and Rishis who passed by these caves and meditated here including Swami Ram Dass of Kerala who stayed here. Swami Ram Tirath also visited this place.

The Guru of Swami Purashottam and Swami Bhramanand ji Maharaj of the Sri Rama Krishna Math Calcutta.

The ashram is a heaven, peaceful, calm and full of divine energy of the Vaishisth era. The ganges flows past the holy caves.

Baba Dulo Sugan

Ancestors of Jarmani Dass had their guru who blessed the Dhir family with luck, prosperity, means and protection. He also lived at the Dewan Daulat Ram Haveli, near Jalaw Khanna, Kapurthala. On the left hand corner of the five storey Haweli, his room had a well too. After Babas demise his wooden shoes are still there and at night one can clearly hear his Khavavas Sound walking is his room. Daily water was changed in the morning for his prayers in a copper Lota. Unfortunately this Haveli was sold by Sushila Devi.

However whoever covers the Old Well, in that portion of the Haveli might face ill-luck. As Baba's abode is still there.

Some forget old customs and family traditions unfortunately.

Social Engineer

"Life worth living is the life lived for others."

A. S. Vatni

At the partition of the country in August, 1947, bloody communal riots broke out on an unprecedented scale. Long caravans of refugees began to cross the border from both the sides. The sick and the wounded were in immediate need for help and the able bodied were in need of rehabilitation. Diwan Jarmani Dass's heart bled at the sight of the uprooted millions hurrying to cross the border. All his life he had been a doughty champion of secularism. He felt very sad when he saw Hindus and Muslims slitting each others throat. He helped the wounded with shelter, clothes and money, and those who were injured were admitted to hospitals and treated at his expense. He distributed vests worth Rs. 20,000 at different camps.

As early as August 1948 Shri Mehar Chand Khanna, the Minister In-charge of the Union Ministry of Relief and Rehabilitation, New Delhi, requested Jarmani Dass to join the Advisory Committee attached to his Ministry for consultation. He agreed to his request. Other members of the Committee were Mrs. Sucheta Kripalani, Diwan Bhanju Ram Gandhi, Lala Achint Ram, S. S. Ujjal Singh, Pandit K. Santhanam, Dr. Dev Raj Narang, Pt. Thakar Das Bhargava, Mr. Sushi Chand, L. Bhimsen Sachhar, Goswami Ganesh Dutt, Dr. Chotithram P. Gidwani, R.S. Parmanand and Sardar Ishar Singh. He realised the importance of funds for rehabilitation work. He persuaded his friends to donate liberally for the noble cause. For augmenting the public funds he formulated lottery scheme and recommended it to the Government. The scheme is detailed below.

The government would organize a lottery with monthly drawings to the grand total of Rs. 1,00,000. The government would sell one million tickets to the public at the nominal value of Rs. 10 each. The drawing would ensure to the investing public through the winning tickets, 70 per cent of the total amount subscribed and the government would retain, at each drawing, 30 per cent profit, that is to say Rs. 30,00,000, In other words, the government would obtain annually for its treasury Rs. 3,36,00,000, which would meet to a large extent the expenses of relieving the poverty of the refugees, without any realisation on the part of the public it was they who had paid this sum.

The organisation, the publicity, the operation and distribution and correct management of a lottery could be entrusted to experienced technicians.

Jarmani Dass can be called a pioneer in the field of rural development. At a time when Ministers hardly thought of peasants, he devoted his time and energy to their upliftment. He came into contact with rural and urban populations of Kapurthala and Patiala and made deep friendship and contacts with the masses in these territories which now occupy a major portion of former Patiala and East Punjab States Union. He knew personally leading lights of the principal villages and towns in Punjab, particularly in the Districts of Kapurthala, Bhatinda, Bamala, Patiala, Kandghat, Solan and Shimla. Because of his love for development work, he was appointed Chairman of the Development Board in Patiala. He was also connected with many boards meant for rural upliftment and development of industries. During his long tenure as Minister in Kapurthala State and later as member of the Cabinet in Patiala State when the was in-charge of the portfolios of Agriculture Industries, Forests, Sanitation, Health, Garage and Commerce, Jarmani Dass brought many educational and medical institutions into existence.

He founded orphanages and sports clubs, many of which are still in existence. At Kapurthala, he formed a Shri Sudharani Sabha at the behest of his eldest brother Diwan Sureshwer Dass. This body-building club is still in existence. He took active part in organising cattle fairs and exhibition in Patiala State. The X-Ray institution and other similar institutions were established at his suggestion at Patiala and other places in the State. As Chairman of the Development Board, he brought into existence many buildings and new roads . He also organised Ayurvedic Institutions at Patiala on a proper basis. Dairy Farms and Agricultural Model Farms were created through his efforts. Sanitary conditions of the towns and villages were improved as a result of his tireless efforts. During his frequent visits in his official capacity to the villages in Patiala State, he gave relief in every respect to the poor and needy from his private purse, and did his best to improve the lot of the peasants by giving them best seeds and other facilities. He encouraged the co-operative system throughout the State and sanctioned loans. Creation of model farms in different centres of the State gave the peasants true picture as to how they could improve their methods of cultivation and increase their income.

While he was Minister of Agriculture, Commerce, Industries, Health, Forests and Sanitation of the erstwhile princely Patiala State, he was instrumental in negotiating and finalising an agreement with a Bombay business house for the establishment of a Cement Factory at Surajpur now called Bhupindra Cement Works – which is a standing monument to his foresight and enlightened vision. This factory is even now flourishing and giving employment to many and a large revenue to the Government. He had a ropeway set up at Surajpur near Kalka (UP.) He planned similar ropeways at many other places in the State.

These signposts of modern industrialism stand and serve as standing sentinels to his vision and farsightedness. When Acharya Vinoba Bhave, eminent seer, launched his Bhoodan movement, he joined it in a whole-hearted manner and became its active worker. He gave as a gift to this organisation a large tract of land from his ancestral farm at Sultanpur Lodhi in Punjab and encouraged some of his relatives and friends to contribute their quota of gifts of land also towards this noble cause. He undertook a padyatra along with Acharya Vinoba Bhave in Kapurthala to propagate the ideals of the movement.

He was the founder President of this Club which was built at a hill-tip in Loni. From this Club a picturesque view of magnificent pastures all round and of Delhi could be had. It is in this club that people of the West and the East meet to cement the ties of friendship between themselves and their countries. It is because of the historical association of the town that Diwan Sahib chose this site as Headquarters of the club. The town formed part of the five villages which were demanded by King of the Pandavas – Talpat, Sonepat, Bagpat, Loni and Indraprastha in the time of Mahabharata. Loni town, at present a flourishing town, is situated on the Shahdara Saharanpur Road and Ghaziabad on the other side. The name Loni is derived from the Sanskrit. Lavana which means salt. Loni is frequented by Indian and foreign tourists who are attracted to this historic and picturesque town of the epic period. Believed that as Delhi is the capital of such a big country, it is necessary that its major hotels should be organised on the same lines as the great hotels in European and American capitals. They, from the point of view of convenience, equipment, food, services and other standards, etc. should be on the same level as the Ritz and

Carlton Group, the Savoy and Hilton Hotels group and other well-known continental hotels of Paris like the Ritz and George V in Paris. There should also be a club, which should be a suitable meeting place for the ambassadors and other representatives of the foreign countries and officials of the Government of India and the people of the country. The main object of the club as prepared by him was to establish an intimate cultural contact between India and other countries as also the promotion of literature for science and fine arts in this country and abroad, the diffusion of useful knowledge among the members of the club in particular and among the people of India in general. The club could also earn foreign exchange. It was his conviction that such a club combined with a modern Hotel would prove very useful in creating goodwill between the diplomatic corps, foreign visitors to the capital and our own countrymen and women.

At a very early age he realized the importance of having blood banks in the country for the patients particularly poor one. He promoted this idea in the political and official circles and at the first available opportunity established a blood bank in Delhi and became its Chairman. Many conferences were held at different places in New Delhi under the Chairmanship of Dr. Rajendra Prasad when he was Food and Agriculture Minister of the Government of India and Dr. Pattabhi Sitarammayya, Governor, Madhya Pradesh. Other patrons included Mrs. Indira Gandhi, Shri A.B. Pandit, Major General S.S. Sokhery, etc. In this institutions, free blood was supplied to the poor without which they had no chance to survive in case of serious operation or disease. Dr. Rajendra Prasad in one of his speeches appreciated Diwan Sahib's work in this particularly charitable institutions. Both Dr. Rajendra Prasad and Dr. Pattabhi Sitaramayya were extensively quoted by the press.

Other office-bearers included Shri B.K.P. Sinha and Shri R.S. Sinha, M.P., Shri C.D. Pandey, M.P. and Shri R.S. Pandey, M.P. Shri V.C. Shukla, the then Union Minister for Information and Broadcasting, the Cultural Counselor of the French Embassy, Shri D.R. Sondhi and Dr. Dev Raj Narang, Business Magnate, Shri M. Bhattacharjee, Manager, United Commercial Bank, Parliament Street, New Delhi and Kumari Sona Bhutani. The speeches delivered by Jarmani Dass in French were always applauded by the audience, particularly the French.

Taxis in Delhi before 1947 did not have meters. This frequently led to unpleasant situations. The taxi drivers loved to ply their taxis on flat rates. His innovative mind led to the introduction of a metered Taxi Service which became a source of annoyance to the unscrupulous taxi operators. It gave lot of relief to the public and revenue to the Government. The "POP" flag type meters were imported from France by Diwan Jarmani Dass.

He was the leading light of the Samaj. As Chairman of the Delhi Advisory Committee, he along with Shri Gulzari Lal Nanda, the then Union Home Minister helped the Samaj greatly. Its office was located at 22 Sardar Patel

Road, (Chankya Puri), New Delhi. Its President was H.M. Swami Gurucharandasji and General Secretary M. Swami Harinarayananandji. He played a great role in the nationalisation of the *"Muths."*

He was the life member of National Sports Club of India, Chelmsford Club and the India International Centre, New Delhi. He was founder member of Cricket Club of India, Brabourne Stadium, Bombay. In 1954 a reception committee was formed to celebrate the birthday of Pandit Jawaharlal Nehru, the first Prime Minister of Independence India, Diwan Jarmani Dass agreed to become its Chairman. At a function held on November 14, 1954, under the Presidentship of Sardar K.M. Panikkar, Diwan Jarmani Dass read out his speech which had been printed for wide distribution.

The speech delivered with mastery and ease is reproduced below:

"Sardar Panikkar, Your Excellencies, Ladies and Gentlemen. It is my proud privilege to welcome you all today in celebrating the auspicious birthday of our beloved Prime Minister, Pandit Jawaharlal Nehru, the architect of modern India.

As I look around in this distinguished audience, I am pleased to see that the representatives not only of the Asiatic countries but also of Eastern and Western European powers and that of the United States of America are present at this function.

Pandit Nehru's birthday is a national festival and his life is most precious not only to India but to the whole world, in creating a causeway of peace and prosperity thought the world. His name will go down in history as a hero who helped to rid the country of hunger and poverty and paved the way for its peace and prosperity in co-operation with the peace-loving nations of the world in accordance with the universally acclaimed policy of Panch Sheel. Lately, Panditji expressed the desire to relieve himself of the onerous burden he carries in guiding the country but the nation cannot lose the services of the best and the noblest man in our country in present times of the country's drive through construction and we pray that he may live long to guide the destiny of India and make this country as one of the most prosperous and powerful thought peace-loving with hoary heritage and material resources. As early as 1917, I had the privilege of meeting Pandit Nehru for the first time and since then this honour has been repeated off and on. When we met only a few months ago at Kapurthala where I was formerly a Minister, he delighted me with a remark with I cherished most in my life, that I was an old friend of his with more than 31 years standing. His amiable ways, personal disposition and sincerity have endeared him not only to those who have known him for so many years but even to those who come into contact with him for the first time. The presence of distinguished diplomats and other distinguished personalities of Delhi in this non-official function is an evidence enough of the respect and esteem he inspires.

Even during the period of 1925-35 when Pandit Nehru was not occupying an official position, his name was one among the most respected personages throughout the world. In my travels around the world even in those early years, his name was on the lips of everyone along with Mahatma Gandhi, the Father of the Nation.

When the Executive Committee was considering the name of distinguished persons to preside over the function, criterion was to select a person who would be as near as possible to our Prime Minister and who could inoculate and articulate the ideals of life and policy of Pandit Jawaharlal Nehru at this function most accurately. The unanimous decision was no body would be more suitable to preside over this function than Sardar K.M. Panikkar who is well known throughout the country and abroad, as a man of integrity, statesmanship and character. Sardar Panikkar has been closely following in to the foot-steps of his leader and his achievements in China, Egypt and in India are much appreciated not merely by the Prime Minister and the Government of India but by the entire country.

Sardar Panikkar and I have been old colleagues and friends. When at Patiala as Foreign Minister, the brilliance and genius of Sardar Panikkar was felt by all his friends and colleagues and prized by the Maharaja Bhupinder Singh of Patiala. Col. Kailash Nath Haksar called him a prodigy in one of his letters to me about twenty years ago. He rose to the highest position in the erstwhile Indian States and moulded the destiny of a number of States as well as during the great Nation making drive towards the integration of States. His scholarly talents are well known and his recent book on Asia is a remarkable contribution to History and International Understanding.

I do not wish to take much of your time in prolonging my speech as you are all anxious to hear the brilliant words from the much talented and eloquent President, Sardar K.M. Panikkar, but I will fail in my duty if I do not say a few words about the aims and objects of this Organisation under whose auspices this function is being held. Though it may look that this Organisation is confined only to Asiatic countries by its name, the main object in developing this Organisation is to spread peace and goodwill throughout the world. With all good citizens of the world we believe that unity which should be amongst the members of a family consisting of a father, mother, sons and daughters, the same unity and friendship should be extended to larger millions of people and then to the whole country, then the same relationship between countries that are our neighbours and further on till the friendship encircles the whole world. In short, the practical objective is to have a sense of brotherly fellowship between nations and nation's people and peoples of different countries throughout so that they may have love for each other in spite of different caste, creed, ideologies and forms of government. This organisation is for peace and goodwill and no better occasion could be found to organise this function than on the birthday of a great man who is a symbol of Peace and Goodwill and to whom we now wish long life and happiness in the service of the motherland as well as to the human world.

Before I resume my seat, Mr. President, I have the pleasure of announcing the decision of the Reception Committee to present a souvenir of gold salver on their behalf to the worthy and much loved Prime Minister as a human token of our heart- felt felicitations on this happy occasion that we are celebrating this evening – the birthday of Pandit Jawaharlal, a name when translated into English means: a jewel, as indeed he is to us to whom be belongs and to the people of the whole world for whose prosperity through peace he uncompromisingly strives every moment of his life."

Diwan Jarmani Dass
New Delhi,
14th November, 1954,
Chairman, Reception Committee

When Mahatma Gandhi died, he organised numerous meetings where resolutions condemning the assassination were passed. He also took the opportunity at this sad occasion of launching a tirade against communalism. His forthright denunciation of cancer of communalism which was vitiating the body politic of the country earned him encomiums from various quarters. All his life he has been a crusader against the canker of communalism, linguistic jingoism, religious fanaticism and provincial parochialism. His deep disdain for the politics of disunity and division and disintegration is too well known to the saner counsels,

Those who have lived in Lahore know that if partition had not overtaken the city, it would have been the Hollywood of East. There was on lot of talent, beauty, capital and enterprise available in Lahore that it only required a wise move from some knowledgeable person to start the film industry. This step was taken by Jarmani Dass who was the first to start film making on sound lines. The name of his concern was Oriental Talkies which produced several films. As one would expect the most successful of his films was 'Sacred Ganges'. He had earlier visited the studios at Hollywood. His experience and observation had their impact on 'Sacred Ganges'.

The Ministry of Relief and Rehabilitation at the Centre had opened work centres at many places in Delhi – Jamuna Hosiery Factory at Turkaman Gate and Handicraft Centre at Kingsway Camp and in Punjab – Sudhas Nilokheri, Ludhiana – for rehabilitating the large numbers of refugees who had concentrated in the towns of Northern India. At the request of the Secretary of the Ministry, he visited the work centres and gave his report to the Government. He made use of his wide contact in India and abroad and met Commercial Attaches of various embassies in Delhi and also contacted business houses abroad to ascertain what products they would buy from these centres. On going around these centres he found that the products were not good enough to be exported. He found that women participation in cottage industry was much less than the desired level. He suggested the inclusion of new products and new designs. He took a round of the centres along with trade commissioners and commercial attaches of the various embassies in Delhi and identified the products that would be exported. These items included Phulkaries, Carpets, Calico printing, Embroïdery work, Leather novelties, etc. He in a sense was promoter and lover of arts and crafts, a friend of artists, nay, a finest flower of culture and civilization. His contribution in the realm of cottage and village industries is commendable in Patiala State.

Diwan Jarmani Dass

Great are those who harness the tides and eddying form of change rather than sucumb to them. Not afraid to challenge, pristine Gods or make interventions in time-honoured customs they themselves become the motivating forces of change, rejuvenation and rebirth. The life and living of the late legendary figure personified in Diwan Jarmani Dass, an able and astute administrator, a front-ranking Minister in the erstwhile princely states of Kapurthala and Patiala, a simple and suave diplomat, a sterling sportsman, an ardent social worker and staunch reformist and nationalist all rolled into one who strode on the stage of the 20th century leaving a blazing trail behind is no exception to this rule.

During his Ministership in charge of Agriculture, Industries, Forests and Sanitation in the erstwhile princely order of Kapurthala Land Patiala States – Diwan Jarmani Dass was responsible for opening countless medical and educational institutions, orphanages and welfare centres which brought solace and succour to society. Shri Sudharani Sabha at Kapurthala, founded by Sureshwer Dass, the then

Chief Justice of Kapurthala state continuing till today and to which he contributed a lot is a standing citadel of welfare work done by him.

That he contributed for 15 years whole of his pension from Kapurthala state and large amount of money from his own pocket towards funds connected with the national activities can be corroborated from the leading local lights of Indian National Congress. His unstained and unequivocal support to national cause earned him the wrath and displeasure of the powers. He originated the idea of establishing a legislature in Kapurthala state and on his advice Maharaja Jagjit Singh of Kapurthala issued orders for the formation of a Legislative Assembly in the state of Kapurthala much to the chagrin and vehement opposition of the Chief Minister of Kapurthala state.

The effervescence and growth of social, medical welfare and developmental activities in the princely Patiala State emanated from the policies and programmes which he formulated and carried out as Minister of Agriculture and Industries in the Cabinet. The Model Farms are resounding testimony of his vision, statesmanship and administrative acumen. Not only this, the milk of human kindness flowed profusely in his Himalayan.

Diwan Sahib gave relief from his private purse to the general run of humanity and especially the peasant. He also gave maintenance allowance to several widows and disabled at Kapurthala & Sultanpur Lodhi till 1957.

The relief and rehabilitation work undertaken by him during the partition in 1947 speaks volume about his philanthropy and political sagacity. Many a wounded were treated at Dr. Lall's Nursing Home, 4 Pusa Road, New Delhi. Diwan Sahib contributed huge sums of money to this nursing home and thus saved many precious lies.

He was also Chief Promoter and Chairman of the Blood Bank in Delhi which supplied free blood to the needy. Many a meeting of this Blood Bank were Chaired by Dr. Rajan Babu (then Minister of Food and Agriculture) and also by Patlabhi Sitaramayya, the official historian of the Indian National Congress. The laudable work done by this life saving institution was amply appreciated by Dr. Rajendra Prasad as well as Dr. P. Sitaramayya and widely reported in the press.

He also served as chairman, All India Blood Donation Society which has branches throughout India.

As member, Advisory Committee, Relief and Rehabilitation (other members were Sarvarhur Bakshi, Tek Chand, Bhimsen Sachhar, Sardar Ujjal Singh) he distributed free clothes, and vests.

Jarmani Dass was pioneer in the introduction of "POP", French metered taxi service in Delhi by the name of R.B. Taxi Service, much to the annoyance of taxi drivers.

A former secretary of the Chamber of Princes, Jarmani Dass, the scion of a great family, was born on October 4, 1895. He was from a noble and illustrious family of reformers of Kapurthala state whose ancestors not only held coveted positions in the said state but fervently fought against social ills and taboos and brought reforms in martial and dowry systems.

This led him to enroll himself as Member of Indian National Congress in 1917 on his return from educational and academic fields of Oxford and Paris. As delegate to the RTC in London in 1930-31 on behalf of Indian states, he took up an independent national view, and espoused the cause of Indian independence. Here he had the privilege to meet Mahatama Gandhi who applauded his speeches at the RTC.

He was one of the founder member of the first Managing Comittee of Alliance Francaise de Delhi. Later, was President too. Due to his prolific background of French language and literature and a first hand knowledge of France, he was often called in diplomatic and social circles as the "Frenchman of India". Even during his Ministership the French Government adorned him with its accolade of the legend of honour of France. It was the culmination of the cause of Indo-French friendship.

As a profile writer and seasoned author the name of Diwan Jarmani Dass is a household word especially after the publication of his monumental work entitled *Maharaja.* This best seller and later *Maharani,* throw a concentrated beam of light on the kings and rulers of the former princely order. The book *Maharaja* generated a stormy debate and its references reverberated in the Parliament of India. Smt. Sushila Jarmani Dass and Rakesh, ardent social workers, philanthropists and humanists continue to live at Mansingh Road, New Delhi.

•••

Diwan Daulat Ram – the father of Jarmani Dass

One of the Rani's of Kapurthala

Rani Sita Devi

Rani Kapurthala

Jarmani Dass &
Anita Delgado

METRO-GOLDWYN-MAYER
STUDIOS

CULVER CITY, CALIFORNIA

10/16/29

Sardar Iramani Dass,
Military Secretary to
His Highness, the Maharajah of Kapurthala.

Sir:

The bearer, who hands you this at Pasadena is Mr.Barrett Kiesling of our organization, whose services will be at your disposal during your visit to Los Angeles.

Mr.Mayer's program, arranged with Major Bowes, is as follows:

Upon your arrival in Los Angeles your party will be met by Mr. Mayer, Mr.Grauman and a delegation including the press.

Under motor-cycle police escort you will be taken to the Roosevelt Hotel where a dinner will await you in your rooms. (It is my understanding that your party will dress for the evening on the train, before arrival.)

Your party will then be taken to the Western (formal) Premiere of our newest production, "Hallelujah" at the Fox Palace Theatre. Tickets for His Highness' personal attendants will be provided as requested.

Following the performance you will be taken to the Blossom Room of the Roosevelt Hotel for supper and dance. One hundred motion picture celebrities will attend.

Tomorrow, Thursday, Mr.Kiesling will escort your party to the Universal Studio where you are expected for lunch between twelve and twelve-thirty. At two-thirty you will leave Universal Studios for the Metro-Goldwyn-Mayer Studios where His Highness will meet motion picture celebrities at tea and where a program of entertainment has been arranged.

The most interesting routes will be taken in order to disclose to His Highness, the interesting points in this vicinity.

At the Roosevelt your party will occupy the personal suite of Mr.Joseph M.Schenck.

You will have motor-cycle police escort during your entire visit here.

Programme of HHK and Jarmani Dass in MGM studios, Hollywood

METRO-GOLDWYN-MAYER STUDIOS

CULVER CITY, CALIFORNIA

-2-

You will be returned to your hotel tomorrow in ample time for dinner and then taken to train for San Francisco.

Trusting this meets with your approval and with best wishes, I am,

Cordially,

Pete Smith

Director of Publicity.

NO AGREEMENT OR ORDER WILL BE BINDING ON THIS CORPORATION UNLESS IN WRITING AND SIGNED BY AN OFFICER

Programme of HHK and Jarmani Dass in MGM studios, Hollywood

H H Kapurthala in Hollywood with Jarmani Dass

H H Kapurthala in Hollywood with Jarmani Dass

A foreign Rani of Kapurthala

Jarmani Dass & friend

Jarmani Dass & Anita Delgado with her sister

Invitation to the reception of His Majesty, the King of Egypt in 1927

HH Kapurthala on a trip by sea in a P & O company liner

Jarmani Dass & H H Kapurthala in Europe

Jarmani Dass in Paris with a friend

A caricature of
Jarmani Das